The Riding Devil bikers advanced, chewing up Able with wild gunfire

Gadgets tried again to contact Lyons, but a bullet tore the small radio communicator from his hand.

The team pounded up the concrete ramp. "Right to the top. We don't want them to flank us," Blancanales barked.

The ominous roar of powerful motorcycles came from the parking lot the trio had just abandoned.

Pol watched as the riders wheeled into the garage, each one clutching a handgun. They rode in single file, moving slowly. Blancanales knew there were more bikers in the area, but he couldn't pinpoint where—the noise of the bikes in the garage was deafening.

The Able Team ace had a hunch that the building was surrounded, that the eight men inside were just the stopper in the bottle....

ABLE TEAM

Five Rings of Fire

Dick Stivers

A GOLD EAGLE BOOK FROM

W🌐RLDWIDE

TORONTO · NEW YORK · LONDON · PARIS
AMSTERDAM · STOCKHOLM · HAMBURG
ATHENS · MILAN · TOKYO · SYDNEY

First edition April 1984

ISBN 0-373-61211-7

Special thanks and acknowledgment to
Tom Arnett for his contributions to this work.

Printed in Canada

1

Tracy Shaw, a four-foot slip of a girl, stood erect on the balance beam. Chalk, a dusty reminder of an earlier workout on the bars, covered parts of her sky-blue body suit. The suit hugged her sinewy frame with the familiarity of a longtime friend. She stood with poise, her back slightly arched, in a sensual meeting of body and athletics.

She had blocked from her mind every dull inch of her surroundings—the women's gymnasium at the University of California at Los Angeles. Concentration gripped her youthful face. Over and over her mind repeated instructions that had been drilled into her head by her coach.

Over and over the eleven-year-old thought of her goal, the goal of every amateur athlete—Olympic gold. The Games were only five days away.

She was tired. A long day of workouts had zapped the energy she usually possessed. The diminutive gymnast turned her mind from the tired aching in her muscles. She concentrated.

Slowly, treading with the grace born of practice, she walked backward on the beam. Her face remained a mask of concentration, her head tilted slightly skyward. Suddenly, like a cat, the sinewy girl exploded into action.

Blasting off the beam, she arched her spine into a perfect backflip. She was halfway through it when her skull exploded, spewing shards of bone and mutilated brain, the pretty face collapsing into ruin.

And she struck the beam, a slithering, lifeless thing, devoid of grace. For half a heartbeat she was balanced there, then her rag-doll form surrendered to the draw of gravity and collapsed into a viscous, spreading pool of blood.

THE SHOT HAD NOT UTTERED a sound. It had carried out its duty with deadly silence.

Babette Pavlovski, a Czechoslovakian defector and coach of the U.S. women's gymnastic team, gagged at the sight of the young girl being shot. Pavlovski and America's top hope for a gold medal, Ellie Kay King, had been spotting for the girl in the otherwise empty gym. King, nicknamed Kelly, threw up.

Just inside the gymnasium's main doors, two FBI guards—stationed to protect the defector—lay on the floor, staring at the ceiling. Bullet holes had left punctures in their faces.

Ten feet from the doors stood two gunmen. They wore ragged jeans and UCLA sweatshirts to blend in with the fashion at the school's main campus. Each carried a gym bag over his shoulder—a bag for carrying the tools of death, handguns with large cylinders planted on the ends of the barrels. Both handguns were pointed squarely at the face of Babette, the target for the first misplaced shot.

In the time it took Tracy Shaw to drop in a heap, Babette Pavlovski reacted. Shots rang out. The coach launched her long body under the beam, bowling Kelly over. The shots missed their mark by inches. Kelly and the coach rolled together, taking refuge behind a wooden vaulting horse.

Babette spoke rapidly to her star black gymnast.

"They're after me, but they'll kill every witness they find. I'll make them follow me away from here. Phone this number." She handed Kelly a piece of paper. "Tell whoever answers exactly what happened...and tell them to get some help for Tracy. I...I think it's too late."

Babette sprang into a sprint, zigzagging toward another exit. Small, nearly silent coughs of gunfire followed her moves. None connected.

When she reached the junction of the corridor, she paused long enough to ensure that her pursuers saw her. As she turned the corner, a bullet chipped the wall just inches behind her.

Meanwhile Kelly made her way back to Tracy. Kelly was in shock. She took one look at her teammate and gagged again. She knew the young gymnast was dead. She dashed to the director's office to use the phone.

Brenda Gillium and JoJo Tate, two young gymnasts who had witnessed the carnage from a dressing-room window that faced the gymnasium, followed Kelly into the director's office.

"There's one outside," Brenda hissed to Kelly. "We saw him. There's one outside."

"Sleepy" Sam Spanier stood nervously outside the gymnasium door. His hand sweated streams as he grasped the silenced Makarov inside his gym bag.

Sleepy was not new to the exterminating game. But this time around he was unsure of his client and his information. The Riding Devils had been doing muscle work, plus the occasional "removal" for the Mafia since the Devils had lost most of its force about a year earlier. The mob was okay to work for, but this new client. . . .

The new guy said he was German, but that was bullshit. Sleepy's old lady was German and she didn't talk like the client.

The door to the gymnasium swung open. Sleepy checked to make certain the hall was still clear. He saw a couple of kids but they were heading the opposite way.

He turned his head away for an instant and when he turned it back he saw one of the kids running at him faster than he thought a little girl could run. He started to pull his weapon from the bag.

Before he could get the gun free, Brenda Gillium was airborne, her body curled in a crouch. Sleepy watched in helpless horror as the young cannonball hurtled at his head.

At the last possible second, the girl's legs shot out and smashed him in the face. The back of his head hit the wall behind him. He felt bone crush. Blood sprayed. He felt his life leave his body.

Never again would he feel anything else.

2

Rosario "Politician" Blancanales and Hermann "Gadgets" Schwarz sprinted through the drizzle. They were headed for a black executive jet that was coming to a stop by a freight terminal at Holman Field, St. Paul. The logo on the side of the jet read: ABLE GROUP, Security Services.

The plane stopped, a door lifted and stairs were dropped to the ground. Blancanales and Schwarz boarded.

Carl Lyons, the third member of Able Team, stood just inside the entry. He greeted his teammates with rabbit punches to their shoulders.

The three justice warriors from Stony Man Farm had escaped a sacrificial slaughter in the lair of a smugglers' broker called The Dragon, tens of thousands of feet up in the Hindu Kush. It was one helluva close call. And it was a story that would stay buried, too tangled in bloodcurdling treachery to be retold.

Few words were exchanged between the men. They had fought together, nearly died together—words fell short of what they felt about one another. They convened around a small conference table as the plane taxied for runway space.

"Love that logo on this souped-up flybox," Schwarz said. "We sure didn't have trouble recognizing the right plane."

"Where're the S.M. boys?" Blancanales asked.

"The big Stony Man guns are up to their asses in trouble. This one's our baby. We're on our own," Lyons informed them.

"Sweet shit," Blancanales said, a smile on his face. "What's the action?"

"In less than two hours," Lyons said, "we'll be up to our butts in local and international politics. But don't worry—I've become a diplomat. I can handle politics like a pro."

"What's this political crap?" Gadgets demanded. "You're about as good at politics as I am at catching lead in my teeth."

"Job still has to be done. Order came directly from the Oval Office."

Lyons produced two eight-by-ten photographs. "We've got some shapely compensation on this trip." He handed them the pictures. "The tall Caucasian is Babette Pavlovski. She's one of the athletes Mack Bolan rescued when he destroyed the Zwilling Horde. She's a defector from Czechoslovakia. Someone tried to kill her this morning, killed a kid gymnast instead. Also got Pavlovski's two FBI bodyguards.

"The young black is Ellie Kay King, known as Kelly. She's our best bet for gold at the Olympics. Pavlovski's been coaching the team since she defected two years ago. It was King who called Stony Man Farm and told them what happened."

"They're not tough to look at," Gadgets commented.

"Wait'll you see them move," Lyons snapped.

"How the hell did an athlete have a telephone number for Stony Man?" Blancanales asked. "Someone hand out Stony Man business cards?"

Lyons grinned in spite of himself. "Pavlovski wrote a letter to Sergeant Grendal, care of the Director of Central Intelligence. Grendal was the only name she knew Mack by. In the letter she said there's a lot of pressure being placed on black American athletes to head to Communist countries after the Games. Brognola talked to her, gave her the Stony Man number, then talked to the FBI to make sure things were handled right. Pavlovski must have passed the number to King.

"Brognola's in some sort of deep shit right now, so he called me, briefed me, and here I am delivering this fucking masterful briefing to you clowns. The FBI's going to meet us at LAX and give us any more intel they may have stumbled upon."

Politician shook his head. "The FBI's officially in charge of Olympic security—they've probably got an army of Feds. And LAPD's probably got its finest out there. So why us?"

"Three reasons," Lyons said. "First, the President is afraid this is a major terrorist offensive. Second, there's a lot of political fighting going on between LAPD, the FBI and the sheriff's office over control of Olympic security—the prez wants some outsiders to coordinate things. And third, the U.S. has a lot at stake. Pavlovski is a defector. She was supposed to be protected. We don't know why her security failed, but if the KGB—that's who they figure's after her—can bump off defectors on U.S. soil, there isn't a country around that's going to take us seriously. And, while we can't stop people from leaving this free country of ours, we can stop people from pressuring them to leave.

"Ellie King will be with the FBI agent at the airport," Carl continued. "We'll get filled in on the way to UCLA. Then we'll grab Pavlovski, discover what sort of tactics the KGB's using to pressure the blacks and wrap it up in time for lunch."

"Miracles," Gadgets said, rolling his eyes heavenward.

Lyons got up and heaved two heavy wooden cases and one suitcase onto the table. He dumped out the contents of the suitcase.

"Special underwear from NASA to you," Lyons said, holding up what looked like long johns with no sleeves and short legs. Heavy plates could be seen through the material.

"Just what we need in the heat of L.A.," Pol said, "long underwear. I'd rather get shot than sweat to death."

Lyons ignored the complaints. "Pay attention. I'm only going over this once. These are Kevlar on the outside. The Velcro-fastened pockets hold ceramic trauma plates. The inside is what NASA invented—it's full of micro tubing. The fluid is pumped by a miniature motor that'll keep going on three nine-volt alkaline batteries for twenty-four hours.

"This pouch is the fluid reservoir. You put the small chempacs in there and they'll supply either three hours of heating or cooling depending on which pack you use. It's sweltering in L.A. now, but we're going to be three very cool dudes."

The trio stripped down and donned their outerspace gear. Complaints were tossed about. "We look ridiculous...stupid...." But behind the complaints was the knowledge that the outfits could be lifesavers.

Lyons dipped into one of the cases and produced three breakaway shoulder rigs and three silenced Beretta 93-Rs.

"These go on next," he said. "You'll find pockets on the sides of your vests with extra clips provided."

"You're using a 93-R?" Gadgets questioned. "You prefer a Python."

"Python's a helluva lot better than these popguns, but everything in this mission's been designed to limit any problems during crowd action. You guys also get Ingrams."

"Suppose you're packing a 40mm cannon," Pol said to Lyons.

"Damn right," he said, holding up an M-203 with an M-16 barrel and an M-79 grenade launcher in an over/under configuration. "We've got smokes, tear gas, HE and puke gas to use."

Politician, rifling through the cases, came up with some new death distributors. "Nice stuff," he said. "Damn nice stuff."

"They're custom made," Lyons said. "Take .458

Winchester Magnums. If we're forced to snipe, I doubt we could find a better piece to use. The sport shirts are to conceal this armor.''

"Not a bad fit," Gadgets declared as he slipped the shirt on.

"We land in twenty minutes," Lyons announced.

3

Lyons, Schwarz and Blancanales stretched as they made their way off the jet at LAX. Bright sunshine greeted their eyes as they stepped down the ladder. A man and a woman stood waiting for them beside a station wagon.

"Nice," Lyons crooned, looking at the female half of the duo.

"Lacks meat," Gadgets said, not bothering to suppress a monster yawn. "I like my women with a little something you can hold on to."

The man stood surveying Able Team. He was a Caucasian with a slightly rounded face and a fit body wrapped in a lightweight gray suit. He looked like an accountant. He was a field agent. His short-fingered blunt hand reached out as Able Team came near.

"Identification please."

"Want a look at a mole on my ass?" Lyons asked.

The agent fell short of being amused. "ID *please*."

Lyons pulled a wallet from his hip pocket and produced a wrinkled envelope, which he handed to the agent. The man in gray extracted a single page, then read it.

"Okay," the agent said, obviously impressed with the President's signature anchoring the page. "What's next, sir?"

"First," Lyons informed him. "Cut the 'sir' crap. Call me Carl, or Lyons."

"Sheldon Archer, L.A. Bureau Chief," the agent said.

"My partners, Gadgets and Politician," Lyons said, introducing Schwarz and Blancanales.

Archer turned to the black woman standing behind him and introduced her. "This is Miss King."

Kelly said hello to the man, then informed them that she was at the airport to meet another plane. "It's been in for ten minutes. I want to talk to one of the passengers—a man I met at an international meet in Montreal." Her voice was heavy. She was still shaken over the loss of her teammate.

"Let's go," Lyons said as the men of Able Team tossed their wooden cases and suitcases into the back of the wagon and then climbed in. Archer drove them to the upper-level roadway and to the west end of the complex where the new international terminal was located.

"Look at all the reporters," Pol said as they approached an old school bus that was being loaded with young black athletes. "Whenever athletes arrive in this country the news hounds are there."

"The athletes are already boarding the bus," Kelly said. "Let me out."

Archer pulled up in front of the bus and King scrambled out. The four men followed her.

A tall blond man in a suit confronted Archer.

"You can't park here," he barked. "Move that heap."

A television reporter, sensing some drama in this small confrontation, zeroed in on the blond man, jerking her cameraman along.

"That's Petra Dix," Politician said. "She does the night news on one of the networks."

Archer moved in front of the station wagon to meet the shouting man. Dix closed in on the controversy.

In a breath, the members of Able Team sensed something was wrong. The big blond man moved too smoothly. The scene was all wrong.

They scanned the area. American guides outnumbered athletes. The guides were all burly white males, with muscles attached to muscles. Three of the heavies held members of the press away from the athletes while others corralled the Africans onto the bus.

Ellie King sized up the situation. She ran around in back of the bus, avoided two guides and slipped onto the vehicle with the other blacks.

One of the guides tried to restore order.

"People, the Zambian delegation is late for a special reception we've set up for them. There will be a press conference at the Olympic Village on UCLA's campus tomorrow at 10 A.M. I promise you the biggest story of the Olympics at that time."

"Why are you speaking for the Zambians?" an indignant reporter shouted. "Let them say a few words."

The burly guides began to bulldoze the press away from the athletes.

"Special press conference, my ass," Gadgets said. "Something stinks."

"What are those bastards doing?" Lyons exclaimed. He pointed at three men in gray suits who were roughing up Sheldon Archer. The men had found Archer's credentials. The large blond leader was shouting. Handguns appeared everywhere. Petra Dix, showing incredibly bad timing, stuck her microphone in the face of the head gunman.

"Archer and Dix are boxed in," Lyons said. "Move."

Blancanales straight-armed Dix's cameraman to the ground to get the flunky out of the way.

Able Team attacked.

Sheldon Archer held his own. He grabbed the hand of the top gunman. He forced the hand to give up the gun.

Gadgets took a long flying tackle, knocking Petra Dix to the pavement. He rolled with her, shielding her body with his.

Pol's Beretta whispered at one of the graysuits. He connected with the head. The guncock folded and dropped to the pavement. Politician was wheeling to fire another shot when he was nailed by the 9mm slug of a Makarov. He just grunted. The spacesuit had worked.

The roar of the bus engine grabbed Pol's attention. The vehicle had backed up to get around Archer's station wagon. The Able Team sharpshooter tried to target on the bus tires. He was sent flying by a frightened cameraman fleeing the scene.

Carl Lyons's gun whispered sweet death and another graysuit fell to the ground, his head torn to pieces.

Gadgets did not even take the time to get off the ground before doing his job. He sighted between a pair of thrashing legs and squeezed a shot at a pair of gray legs. The last goon went down with a scream. But the bus had escaped.

Archer and the blond leader were grappling. The blonde landed a few blows to the Fed's face but the latter doggedly hung on. Another blow to the temple knocked Archer to the pavement.

The blonde reached for his gun. Picking it up, he jumped beside a wounded comrade. He pulled a grenade from a pocket. Three Able Team guns coughed. The tall man collapsed in a blood-smeared mess. The wounded man's status dropped to dead. The grenade fell to the roadway, its pin still in place.

Lyons bent and made a fast search of the blond man's pockets. He found a plain business envelope, sealed and addressed to the United States Olympic Committee. He put the envelope in his pants pocket, then retrieved the grenade the gunner had dropped.

"Russian," he said.

He straightened and found himself looking up the business end of a police revolver.

A sheriff's department car was parked on the elevated roadway. Two deputies, guns drawn, came out of the terminal.

"Where were you when the action was going down?" Lyons asked.

"Just put the gun down easy," the deputy replied.

Lyons locked eyes with the policeman, then slowly slid the Beretta back into its holster.

"I said put the gun down," the deputy snapped.

"Put out an all-points on that bus that just pulled out of here," Lyons ordered.

"Why the hell would I do that?" the officer spat.

Lyons glanced at the reporters who, regaining their courage, were starting to get up from the turf where they had thrown themselves when the shooting started. He did not want to answer any questions within their hearing.

Archer bent to retrieve his ID.

"Freeze," one of the deputies on the sidewalk said.

"That's my FBI ID," Archer objected.

"How do I know that?" the cop replied. "Try to pick it up and you lose a hand."

"Pick it up, Archer," Lyons said. "I'll show this goof my letter."

Lyons reached for his wallet. The sheriff's man fired. The bullet grazed the left arm of the Able Team member.

Lyons was silent, his eyes narrowed in raging contempt. He continued to pull out the wallet, holding the law officer's eyes with his own, daring the man to plug him with a bullet.

Archer swallowed saliva that wasn't there. He continued to reach for his ID.

Lyons ignored the fire in his arm. By the time the deputy had braced himself to shoot again, the wallet was in sight. Crazy Carl remained cool in his spacesuit; the deputy was sweating buckets. He lowered his gun. His arm was trembling.

Petra Dix, recovering from shock, led the wave of reporters who had stood with wide-eyed amazement at the confrontation between the gutsy Lyons and the cop.

"For crissakes, get footage," she ordered her cameraman.

The man made a move but was stopped by Politician, who shook his head.

Lyons opened his wallet and offered it to the lawman.

"Put it on the ground and back away from it," the officer demanded. "And put your gun down on top of it."

Lyons had taken enough.

In two quick steps he was grabbing the hand holding the revolver. His fist connected solidly with the side of the officer's jaw, dumping him flat on his ass. A quick kick removed the revolver from the man's fist.

"I'll have you for assaulting an officer," the man gasped.

"I'll have you for lunch," Lyons snarled as he booted the man in the ribs and thrust the letter into his face.

"Read it," he said.

Archer, sensing Lyons was now in the driver's seat, took charge. "Try to clear the crowd," he instructed the lawman.

Reporters were firing questions.

"Did someone try to shoot the Zambian athletes?"

"Yeah, but we got here first," Lyons said.

"What happened to the athletes?" another person asked.

"They got on a bus," Lyons snapped.

"Are they okay?"

Lyons held little love for the media. In his mind those involved in journalism were interlopers who always seemed to have their noses in the wrong places. "Ask them tomorrow," Lyons snapped.

By this time another car from the sheriff's department had managed to make it through the crowd and the traffic. The deputies slowly cleared the area of protesting reporters and curious onlookers.

From his seat on the road, the cop finished reading the letter of authority signed by the President.

"Now," Lyons said, speaking softly so that he could not be overheard, "maybe you'll get that all-points out. Athletes have been kidnapped and you're sitting on your ass."

The man ran for his car. He had an urgent message to deliver.

The members of Able Team climbed back into the station wagon and waited for Archer to drive them away. Gadgets dug into the wooden case for spare shells. Blancanales dressed the slight bullet crease on Carl's arm. Lyons opened the letter addressed to the Olympic Committee that he had found on the dead man. He read it and whistled.

"What now?" Archer asked as he started to pull away from the scene.

"Drop us off at UCLA," Lyons said.

He passed the note to Pol. It read:

We are holding the black Zambian athletes until your committee officially recognizes South
Africa. We are sick of your discrimination
against the White Race. If our demand is not
met, the athletes will die.
By order of
The Grand Dragon
of the Invisible Empire

"Damn," Pol said. "Not only the KGB, but now the Ku Klux Klan has entered the picture." He handed the note to Gadgets.

"Some picture," Lyons commented.

4

"It's about time you got here, Fed," the detective said to Sheldon Archer when the car arrived at the UCLA women's gymnasium. He spat the word "Fed" like he was choking on shit.

Archer looked at the square-jawed man. He was tall, lean and wore a white shirt, no tie and a brown suit off the racks of high society. He stood beside a body covered by a sheet.

As Able Team approached, the abrasive man continued, "It's damn hot and I can't do a thing—not even move this stinkin' corpse—until I get permission from some hotshot you're supposed to have with you."

Archer grinned and turned to Carl. "Hotshot, meet Bill Tilden from L.A. homicide."

Tilden looked at Lyons, obvious disdain in his eyes.

Neither man offered to shake the other's hand.

"We've met," Lyons told the FBI man.

"This is one of the gun punks," Tilden said. "Had his head kicked in by some little kid gymnast. The other one, the dead girl, has been removed."

He reached down and peeled back the sheet far enough to show the unnatural angle in which the man's head was twisted. He jerked the sheet back up, then straightened and delivered a report in rapid-fire monotone. He sounded like a teletype run amok.

"He's Samuel Spanier, known as Sleepy to other bikers. He rode with the Riding Devils. We've suspected for some time that the Devils have stopped pushing drugs and are into the muscle-and-contract game."

Tilden produced a gym bag. He opened it and showed Able Team the weapon.

"It's been dusted?" Schwarz asked.

Tilden nodded.

Schwarz reached for the gun. He did a quick field strip and continued to examine the piece.

Pol picked up the questioning. "How do you put this case together?"

"Pretty straightforward," Tilden said, shrugging. "Three bikers dressed like students came here. One stayed in the hall to cover their retreat, the other two went into the gym and fired at the coach. A kid got in the way, took a bullet.

"The coach, a woman, had enough brains to go out the other door and let the touch-men follow her. We've got no idea if they got her or not. We've got a pickup out on the entire gang."

He paused and nudged the corpse with his toe. "This one had his neck broken by a little kid. She came charging out of the gym and damn near kicked his head off."

"A girl did that?" Gadgets exclaimed.

Tilden nodded.

"Good for her," Lyons said.

Lyons began to walk away from Tilden, the other members of Able Team following him.

"What about the body, hotshot?" Tilden said, more than a little annoyed at having to follow orders from Lyons, a man he had run into and been shown up by a number of times.

"Move it. Worship it. Stick it for all I care."

As Archer made a move to follow Able Team into the gym, Tilden grabbed his arm.

"What's that son of a bitch got to do with this case?"

"He's direct from the President. He's the boss."

Tilden groaned.

The group entered a room adjoining the gym. Pol turned to Lyons and said, "We've got to decide what to tell the press. Any major leak of this and we could blow everything. Any suggestions?"

"This part is easy," Gadgets said. "It's the kidnapping that's going to be hard."

"For this action here," Pol said, "we just won't mention the type of gun and we won't speculate on the motives. We'll just say members of a motorcycle gang came in here and shot the place up. One of the gymnasts caught a bullet."

"That should do it," Lyons intoned. "The press will eat it up, though. Kid gymnast murdered. In cold blood. Film at eleven."

"We'll get everyone to go along with that," Pol said. "But we have to get the police on the abducted Zambians. If the kidnapping hits the papers, the shit hits the fan."

"And we get most of it blown in our faces," Lyons said.

"I can take care of that for now," Archer volunteered. "We have ways of keeping kidnappings quiet for a while."

With strategy mapped out, Able Team was ready to roll; Lyons was itching for action.

"What the hell are we waiting for then?" he said. "Let's get moving. Let's nail this place down tight."

The men moved back into the gymnasium. Tilden had had the body bagged and removed while the foursome discussed the press situation. The FBI had posted new guards to protect the gymnasts, who insisted on practicing despite the fireworks that had erupted earlier.

The four men did a slow survey of the gymnasium and surrounding area, hoping to put an impenetrable lock of security on the campus.

It was Politician who made the recommendations to the Fed in charge of security.

"First, get Ingrams or Uzis in here for everyone on duty. Get extra clips. This short-barreled-revolver crap has gotta go. Second, spread your men around the room some more. If anyone crashes through the doors, these kids are sitting ducks."

Able Team left them to their business. As the men were leaving, a young gymnast, her golden hair fitted into pigtails, came up to Rosario Blancanales, the most fatherly-looking man on the team, and pulled at his shirt.

"You know she'll be back," the petite gymnast said.

"What?" Pol questioned, turning to face the girl. "Who'll be back?"

"Babette. She'll get away from those men and she'll come back here. I know it. She loves us and she worries about us. She's like an old mother hen. She'll be back."

Politician gazed down at the young informant. "You know her that well? You think she'll come back here even though she knows people will be watching for her?"

"She'll be back," the girl said with unbreaking authority.

"Thanks for the tip," Pol said, grinning down at her.

Halfway between the athletes and the door, the four men braked again.

"This isn't adding up," Pol stated. "The snatch at the airport was KGB—professional all the way, but the Klan is claiming responsibility. It wasn't a motorcycle gang—gangs don't work that professionally."

"Yeah," Gadgets agreed. "They were using Makarovs at the gym, though."

Lyons was not paying a whole lot of attention to the conversation. He was still scanning the gym. "If she comes back, it's going to be hard to keep her alive. Hit men are going to be watching for her."

"We'll have to hit the hit men before she shows up," Pol said. "Why don't we get the Feds to supply a sacrificial goat?"

"Hard on the goat," Archer said.

"Fed goats are tough," Lyons said.

5

"I don't think it was such a good idea," commented Gadgets Schwarz.

"What?" questioned Politician.

"To send Lyons on a mission that requires diplomacy. Couth. Tact."

"We didn't send him anywhere. He sent himself. He says Brognola put him in charge and he's bent on proving he can handle it—diplomacy and all."

"You should be handling the politics," Gadgets said.

Blancanales agreed.

The two Able Team warriors had emerged from the women's gym. In the distance to the west was a warmup track, used by athletes and fitness enthusiasts alike.

The pair turned south, walking around the building's front entrance. The sun was blazing hot. Young people were clustered under the few available palm trees. The men of Able Team remained cool in their space-age flak jackets.

Both men carried borrowed gym bags, each of which held an Ingram, spare clips and a few grenades.

"I wonder why so many people are around?" Gadgets said.

"I don't know what's going on. Something doesn't sit right in my gut, and we've got a crowded battlefield if a war breaks out. See anybody, anything suspicious?" Pol asked.

Gadgets shook his head.

"Which way will she come from?" he asked.

They had reached the southeast corner of the building. Pol pointed northeast, over a parking lot, past a parking garage and into a part of campus densely packed with buildings.

The men continued north along the east side of the building. Suddenly, Pol plucked at Gadgets's shirt and pointed, nodding in the same direction.

"That looks like our decoy now."

A woman riding a bicycle emerged from behind the multilevel parking garage and headed toward the gym. The cyclist was only 250 feet from Schwarz and Blancanales. They could make her out clearly.

She wore jeans and a sweat shirt despite the heat of the day. On her head sat the phoniest looking raven-haired wig either man had ever seen. Her feet were covered by gymnast's slippers.

"Quite the stand-in," Pol commented. "Those Feds—"

"Stand-in, hell," Gadgets grunted. "That's the real thing."

The cyclist picked up speed as she pedaled down the hill leading to the gymnasium. One member of a group of "picnickers" pointed her out and shouted.

Hunting rifles, shotguns, handguns from World

War II, even a couple of AR10s, sprouted up all over campus.

Able Team's men exploded into action.

Pol and Gadgets took off toward Babette Pavlovski. Blancanales, pushing his legs to keep up with his young teammate, realized he had no chance of getting to Babette before Gadgets. He pulled up and snatched the Ingram from the gym bag.

Pol picked up at a trot, firing on the move. The modified Ingram spat two-thirds of its thirty-round clip in the second that Pol held down the trigger. The quick slash took out three of the bikers.

Gadgets's sprint had taken every last ounce of push and pull that he could demand from his muscles. He sent his body airborne, in a quarterback-sack, diving position. The timing was perfect. He hit Pavlovski with a flying tackle, knocking her off her bike, taking her to the ground. It was the second time in one long day that the Able Team wizard had been forced to send a woman flying. But he wasn't apologizing, he was saving lives.

Gadgets and Pavlovski rolled. Three .45 chunks of lead nailed him; one slashed into his side, knocking the wind out of him. And under him, Babette struggled, thinking that the man who had jolted her off the bicycle was an enemy.

As bullets rang off Gadgets's gear, he tried to comfort her with the whispered words, "Easy... easy." Finally the gymnastics coach realized the man on top of her was an ally. They kept rolling, then they crawled for cover, stopping behind a metal bike rack.

Politician covered their moves. He emptied the rest of the Ingram's clip, spraying as wide an area as possible. His shots were rewarded with a few screams of searing pain. The would-be assassins scrambled for cover. By the time Pol reached Gadgets and Babette, both were on their feet in a combat crouch.

Babette turned to Schwarz.

"Tracy. Tracy Shaw. Is she okay? Is she...?"

The gymnastics coach began to shake.

Gadgets grabbed her shoulders. "She's dead. I'm sorry. Real sorry."

Babette Pavlovski felt sick. She listened to the man trying to comfort her.

"Listen. We can't stop here. We've gotta move or we'll get killed. Babette, fight. Fight for Tracy."

Gadgets started to yank the Ingram from the gym bag, but Babette grabbed it from his grip. He let her have it. She had decided to fight for her fallen pupil. He pulled the Beretta from its shoulder rig and quickly detached the silencer.

The trio knew their stay behind the bike stand had to be shortlived. Cover was minimal. Manpower was lacking. The assassins began firing again.

Pol fired short bursts that tore at flesh, discouraging the enemy from moving closer. Gadgets did a quick recon.

"Through the parking lot," he said. "We'll make a stand in the garage."

Babette started firing short bursts. Each found a target. The three whirled and were off, zigzagging toward the parking lot. Gadgets used the Beretta, snapping single shots as he ran, keeping enemy heads low.

They paused behind two cars in the parking lot, careful to keep their legs and feet behind tires. The enemy dispatched pincer forces around the buildings.

Gadgets handed Babette more clips. "Let's get out of here before they flank us," he instructed.

As they weaved between the cars, making for the garage, Gadgets pulled a small radio from his belt.

"Wizard to Ironman. Wizard to Ironman."

Ironman Lyons did not answer.

AFTER LEAVING POL AND GADGETS, Archer drove Lyons to the FBI office on Wilshire Boulevard. Lyons had little use for the organization, but he knew that in this mission it was necessary. While Able Team might be able to accomplish its task without outside help, they would definitely need outside cooperation.

With Archer acting as a mediator, Lyons got his point across in no time at all. He had the FBI's backing. Archer stayed at the FBI headquarters to arrange for a Babette double and to coordinate the press release on the gymnast's murder and the blackout on the kidnapping. Lyons went on to the LAPD where, in what seemed to be a lifetime ago, a previous lifetime, it seemed—he had been a sergeant.

As he walked into the familiar building he felt the emotion that always rose in his gut when he thought of cops—sympathy. He could sympathize with the job those poor bastards were asked to perform day in, day out. What he couldn't stand about the LAPD was the bullshit and the red tape that choked the entire operation.

Lyons stopped at the front desk and questioned the desk sergeant.

"Captain Braddock around?"

"It's Chief Braddock now, Carl," the desk sergeant answered. "A lot of changes have been made since your days."

Lyons did a double take when the man behind the desk spoke. "Len Terney," Lyons exclaimed, recognizing the face. "Gone from beat cop to desk jockey."

Terney smiled. "A man gets too old to tear shoe leather. It'll happen to you some day."

The two men shook hands.

"I hear you've been in here a bit," Terney said. "Guess I just keep missing you. It's been a long time since we teamed up."

"Long time," Lyons agreed. "Braddock here?"

"I don't think you want to see him. He's in a terrible mood."

"I'm not revolving my life around old Braddock's moods."

"Same old Lyons," Terney said.

"I've gotta see him, Len. It's a business call."

The sergeant shrugged and picked up one of the telephones on his desk. He dialed a three-digit number.

"Carl Lyons to see you, Chief. He says it's business." The sergeant shouldered a long pause before speaking. "Yes, sir. I'll tell him."

Around LAPD, Lyons had a reputation as a damn fine warrior, but certain upper-echelon heads hated his brashness, his arrogance and his incurable inability to conform. Braddock was one of those heads.

"Ah, Carl. The chief says to say hello, but he's busy. He told me to take care of what you want—"

"Shit," Lyons spat as he turned and headed toward Braddock's office.

"Don't do it, Carl. I'd have to stop you."

Lyons wheeled, reached in his wallet and handed Terney the letter from the President.

"It's a little worn," he said. "Overuse."

Terney whistled. "God. Is this for real?"

Lyons nodded. He took the letter back and put it in his wallet.

"I'll call him again," Terney said.

"Don't bother," Lyons said as he headed toward Braddock's office.

A young policewoman sat at the desk in front of the chief's office. She was tall and well built with shiny blond hair and a healthy glow. Her eyes had strength. Strength to hold a man. The name on the desk plaque read Nel Bly.

As Lyons approached, Officer Bly spoke. "The chief doesn't want to be disturbed."

"Well," Lyons snapped as he strode past her, "I don't want to disturb the chief. I want to talk to him."

"You can't go in there," she said to his back. "The door has an electronic lock. He has to buzz you in."

Lyons felt his temperature rising. Heat took hold of his face. He drove his foot into the office door, connecting just under the handle. The lock mechanism held, but the door jamb shattered. He walked in. Braddock, obviously startled by the uncustomary entrance, was on the phone.

"I think so, your honor," Braddock said. "Listen, I've got to race. Okay. Later." He hung up the receiver.

"Lyons, you fuckup," he growled. "You'd better have a damn good reason for busting into my office. 'Cause if you—"

"Don't get into the threats, Braddock. You'll never back them up. I need your cooperation. I've got a letter—" Lyons wheeled around and saw what he expected to see: Bly, the well-cut policewoman, with a .38 Charter Arms Police Bulldog in her hand pointed at Lyons. She was smart enough to have waited for backup before challenging the Able Team man. The second cop was a black giant in combat fatigues. The monolith held an Uzi in one enormous, beefy hand.

Lyons's radio beeped.

Emergency.

He reached for his belt to answer Gadgets's summons.

"Don't," the female cop cautioned. "Keep your hands clear or lose a hand."

Where have I heard that before? Lyons thought. The four-inch barrel of the .38 was staring at him.

"Braddock," he snapped, "call off the hounds. This beeper, it's an emergency."

Braddock moved out from behind his desk to

confront Lyons. "You think you're something," he said. "Busting in here. Demanding things. You'll sit here, Lyons, until I get some answers."

Lyons's radio beeped again. He turned back to the doorway. Len Terney had joined the party.

"Len. You've got a brain. I've got the governor's backing. The *President's* backing. I've got a letter from the *Man*. You've seen it. Tell him to check it out."

The desk sergeant's voice was weak. "I've got three weeks until retirement. I'm sorry, Carl. I do what the chief says."

The giant in battle fatigues had taken a step back from the others. He still had his right hand wrapped around the Uzi. He had a portable radio in the other hand. He was engaged in a conversation; his voice was low. Lyons figured the guy was calling in reinforcements. Some cops liked to stack the odds.

The Able Team warrior knew the police would be reluctant to shoot if he gave them no reason to—if he didn't threaten anyone. He raised his shirt slowly so that everyone could plainly see he was not reaching for a weapon. He deliberately reached for the radio on his belt.

"Don't," Officer Bly commanded.

Lyons slowly unclipped the radio.

Braddock ordered Terney to take his gun and "other toys."

Lyons moved like lightning, pressing the button.

"Ironman here. Wizard, what's up?"

He was answered by dead silence.

Able Team was in trouble. With Terney nearly on top of him, so was Lyons.

6

Terney reached for the radio. Lyons threw it at the elderly officer's stomach. As the cop moved to deal with the flying object, Lyons popped him with a solid hook in the ribs, knocking him toward the policewoman's .38. The young woman sidestepped to avoid her co-worker. She got set to fire.

Lyons had not pulled his Beretta; a shoot-out would have been suicidal. He had to get someone on his side, if even by force. He made a low dive and hit the woman below the knees, dropping her hard to the floor. Then he felt a monster hand clutch his shoulder.

"Guns away," a voice bellowed.

Lyons looked up. The giant in combat garb was standing over him. "Sorry, Lyons," he said, a sheepish grin crossing his face. "I checked with Archer. You're okay."

"Took you long enough to figure that out," Lyons snarled. "I could be dead meat."

"This isn't exactly my territory," the man explained. "I'm Tim Sanders, Commander, Delta Blue Light Team. That's the code name for an instant-response team the FBI's put together. I'm here with Braddock to coordinate Olympic security."

"Instant response could be a little faster," Lyons said.

Sanders laughed. "I deserve that," he admitted. "Took me a second to contact Archer."

"Who's Archer?" Braddock demanded, fury forming lines across his forehead.

"Archer's a Fed," Lyons said. "Sanders, is your team here?"

"All here for a briefing. Chopper, too."

"My team's in trouble. Can you help?"

"Glad to."

"Let's move," Lyons said.

Lyons was so angry he felt like slamming the door. He couldn't. He had already kicked it in.

Two minutes later, Lyons, Sanders and the men of Delta Blue Light Team were airborne. Lyons gave Sanders a quick briefing.

"I left two men to check on the security of the gymnasts at UCLA. Also, a Babette Pavlovski clone was going to show up and draw the termites out of the woodwork. My men buzzed me. By the time I got to reply, there was no answer."

The specialist nodded.

Lyons brooded.

BABETTE, GADGETS AND POL were weaving toward the brick face of the multilevel parking structure. They snapped shots at the enemy. The Riding Devils advanced, chewing them up the ass with wild gunfire. Gadgets tried again to reach Lyons. A bullet tore the small communicator from his hand.

They ran along the side of the building and turned in the exit ramp.

"Watch the metal spikes," Babette cautioned. "They cut the tires of cars trying to sneak in the exits." Her voice was spliced between deep gasps of breath.

The team stepped over the metal plates and pounded onto the concrete ramp. Pol shot out instructions. "Right to the top. We don't want them to flank us."

The ominous throaty roar of large powerful motorcycles came from the parking lot the trio had just abandoned.

"They won't drive over the spikes," Gadgets said. "They'll come in the entry at the north end of the building. We've got to get to the middle ramp to go to the top."

"You two stop at the first ramp," Politician said, "and cover me. They'll need some slowing down."

The three took off in another sprint, hoping to reach the ramps before the bikers entered the first level. At the first ramp, Babette scrambled partway up, turned and covered Gadgets and Blancanales. Gadgets stopped, crouching behind the wheel of a van. Pol went fifty feet farther before moving behind a parked car, just as the first motorcyclist appeared at the end of the aisle.

Pol watched as eight bikers wheeled into the garage. Each man had a handgun out, ready for action. The bikers rode in single file, moving slowly. Blancanales knew more bikers were in the area but could not pinpoint where—the noise of the bikes in the garage was deafening. The Able Team ace had a hunch that the building was surrounded, that the eight inside were just the stopper in the bottle.

Instinct grabbed at his guts. He turned in time to see a Riding Devil lining him up with an automatic. Pol dropped flat as an entire clip of .45s snapped angrily over his head. He fired a burst under the car at the tire of the lead bike. The tire blew and the rider went down in front of the other bikers. They spread and stopped. Their handguns were up.

The bastard who had fired on him was now edging toward the grounded Able Team member. Rolling and lining up at the same swift instant, Politician laced a burst that tore up the killer's chest. The biker grabbed the area of his heart as hot blood spat wildly from the pulverized organ. Pol rolled back to his original position. Again spotting from underneath the cars, he saw the fallen biker lift his machine off himself as he struggled to rise. He didn't have a chance. Pol triggered his Ingram, and a burst blasted the bastard under the chin. Jawbone collided with brain matter in a gory smear of death.

Reacting with the speed of a man half his age, Politician surged to his feet and sprinted between parked cars and the outside retaining wall. Bullets whistled by him. He stopped behind a car, fired, then moved on. After half a dozen cars, Pol came to a pickup with a high cab. It was backed against the retaining wall, blocking his path. Keeping low, Blancanales moved back toward the center roadway, his legs churning to carry him with speed.

The bikers had all moved past their fallen buddies. Pol took out their new lead rider with a burst to the side. Bullets tore, chewed. The man screamed but his cry was lost in the din. The bikers, caught behind the corpse, stopped. There they waited for the man they felt they had trapped. Pol *was* trapped, but he held the key to freedom.

He reached into the gym bag he had strapped around himself and pulled out two grenades. He let both spoons go and threw one, then the other. The first exploded from its landing pad on the floor, the second burst while it was still in the air.

As the double blast rocked the area, Politician beat a hasty retreat. A quick glance over his shoulder told him that not all the Riding Devils had been leveled by the grenades.

The Able Team warrior brought up the Ingram. It spat one bullet then locked open. Empty clip. There was no time to change clips. No time to draw the Beretta. He turned his will to live into speed. He ran.

Gadgets Schwarz peered around the side of a car he had just taken shelter behind. Two bursts from an Ingram whizzed by him. Looking to one side, he saw Babette sitting on the ramp. She had just fired the machine pistol. A biker was lying under his fallen bike, his weapon still aimed in Gadgets's direction, his face bloodied, eaten by bullets. Gadgets nodded thanks to the female sharpshooter. He then leaned forward and saw Politician running for his life.

The lead biker was set to fire when Gadgets, in a careful two-handed firing stance, let go a single shot. The bullet sailed perfectly, nailing the biker in the hollow of the throat. He went down in a heap, the bike crashing on top of him, crushing the bones of a man already dead.

Blancanales headed for the safety of a parked car. Gadgets held his ground, prepared to meet the two remaining Devils. The bikers had guns raised and were coasting toward him. Thumbing the selector to triple shot, he quickly took care of the biker on the left, dropping him with a solid punch to the chest. Gadgets feinted a move toward the parked cars on the right, then dived to the left. Bullets flew past, inches from his arm. As his body bounced off the garage floor, he fired the Beretta. The bullets connected with deadly results. The man clutched at the remnants of his face. In seconds he was dead.

Gadgets rolled back behind the car. Pol, also behind the shield provided by a car, changed clips. The enemy gave them no time to breathe.

A barrage of bullets announced the arrival of the ground troops who had been scattered around the lawns of the campus.

Blancanales punched a bullet into the eye of one of the bikers attacking on foot. He continued to fire at maximum distance for the Ingram. Two more fell. The rest scattered behind cars. By the time the Devils had defensive positions, Pol and Gadgets were on the offensive.

They borrowed bikes from two of the fallen bikers with the promise of repayment sometime after never.

Gadgets throttled up to where Babette was waiting.

He stopped, giving Pol time to catch up. Gadgets motioned for Babette to swing on the pillion. The feisty woman stayed put, waiting. Gadgets then heard what she was waiting for: more mounted bikers were moving inside.

"To the top," Gadgets screamed.

Pol nodded and took off.

About a minute later the first level was filled with the deafening drone of motorcycles. The bikers raced around the corner of the ramp. Babette sprayed them with the rest of the Ingram's clip then ran and leaped onto the seat behind Gadgets. There were screams of agony as the dead and wounded fell and bikes collided with flesh and bone. Gadgets let the bike loose, leaving carnage and a patch of rubber behind. They drove to the open top-story of the building. Pol was waiting for them at the head of the ramp.

"Babette bought us some time," Gadgets explained.

Babette, her arms wrapped snugly around Gadgets, took a long look at both men.

"Okay," she said. "I've let you tackle me off a bicycle, almost get me killed, take me on this terror mission. Do I get your names?"

"How impolite," Pol said, laughing. "I should have introduced myself between streams of gunfire. Rosario Blancanales. Politician to friends."

"Hermann Schwarz at your service. But since you've got your arms around me, call me Gadgets."

The two men took a calm second out of a stormy battle to drink in the beauty of Babette Pavlovski. The phony wig had fallen off her head during the battle, leaving her short, blond hair looking wild. Her face was shiny with perspiration, but there was a classic beauty that no amount of dishevelment could conceal. And to boot she could fight. Like a soldier.

Pol broke the momentary silence.

"Did you get through to Ironman?"

"No. I lost the radio. Shot out of my hand."

"Then we hold out here until help arrives," Blancanales concluded. "And with this much noise shaking the garage, someone's bound to arrive soon."

"If they come up here," Gadgets said, "they've got to come up these ramps. We should be able to hold them. How much ammo's left?"

A combined count logged four clips for the Ingrams, including the fresh clips in the guns, and seven 15-bullet clips for the Berettas. They also had two grenades.

"We're fine," Pol joked. "We've got six more bullets than there are yahoos out there."

They could hear the thunder made by the Riding Devils biking across the level below them.

"These two bikes are the only cover we've got," Gadgets said. The two men dropped the machines on their sides. The trio flattened out behind them, using the sparse cover to best advantage.

A head soon poked around the corner of the cement ramp. The trio held their fire for a split second and the head jerked back out of sight. The man yelled. "They're holding out at the top."

"I think the party's over," Pol quipped.

"It's just beginning," Gadgets countered as an assault rifle was eased around the curve of the wall, bearing in on the three fighters. Slowly a head followed the rifle around the corner. Politician fired. He put a single shot into an eye.

The sound of cars, their gas pedals pushed toward the floorboard, alerted the trio that trouble was arriving on four wheels.

"Get to one side," Pol instructed Babette. "They'll try to ram our barricade."

Babette drew back from the edge of the ramp and then ran to the side where she could get the longest view of the floor below. She could not yet see the Riding Devils.

Gadgets and Pol each took one of the remaining grenades. Babette, working in perfect tandem with the Able Team duo, shouted "Now!" the second she saw the front of the first car. Gadgets and Politician pulled the pins. They rolled the grenades down the ramps, then sprinted in opposite directions away from the ramps. The car taking the tighter turns was directly over a grenade when it went off. The force of the explosion lifted and twisted the vehicle, leaving it a bent, battered, flaming pile of rubbish that blocked entry from the floor below. The other car made it over the grenade. It charged on toward Able Team's flimsy barricade.

At the last possible moment, the driver of the car saw that there was no one behind the motorcycles.

He swerved sharply to avoid hanging the car up on the bikes. The driver then began a wide sweep that would allow him to stop out of effective firing range or continue to hunt.

Gadgets lined up his Beretta on the rear wheel. Out of the corner of his eye, he spotted a gun barrel emerging from the passenger window. Gadgets let himself collapse to the cold cement as heavy automatic fire blazed over his head.

Blancanales, who had turned a different direction from Schwarz when they had retreated from the ramp, found himself removed from the battle, located behind his partner and at an even greater distance from the pair in the car. He tracked the car with his Ingram, but the range was doubtful and his aim was leading dangerously close to Gadgets. Politician held his fire and began to run toward the action.

Car wheels screeched as the driver used the space on the empty top story to put the vehicle into a power turn and head it back toward Gadgets. The gunner in the car could no longer hit Gadgets without hanging most of his frame out the window. The danger for the Able Team member now lived with the machine that was speeding toward him.

At the bottom of the ramp, the Riding Devils had used a car as a battering ram to remove the burning, beat-up auto. The gunners were now using the car as a shield to get a better angle on, and some protection from, the lone sniper who was preventing them from rushing the ramp. Babette was firing, but was having trouble finding targets. Overhead she heard a large helicopter. She glanced up but the bird had no markings. She turned her attention again to the ramp and opened up the head of a thug who was lining her up over the hood of the car. The man's face was thumped into a bloody pulp.

Instead of getting to his feet and trying to reach cover, Gadgets Schwarz switched the Beretta to full automatic and stitched a line of slugs across the windshield of the car. The instant the gun clicked empty, he rolled to his right as fast and hard as was humanly possible.

The shots killed nothing, but they spiderwebbed the windshield, dropping visibility to nil. The car pulled away to the right as the driver, unable to see the target, veered away from the area where the automatic fire had come from. The skidding back end of the car missed the rolling Able Team member by inches.

The car came to a stop about fifty feet from Gadgets. The door on the far side of the machine opened. The passenger and the driver both got out the same door. Schwarz could see their feet as he shoved another clip into his gun. Remaining prone, the warrior carefully lined up his sights on one of the ankles. Weapons were being swung to bear on him over the top of the car.

Simultaneously, three gunners popped up over the car at the bottom of the ramp. Babette managed to take out one before her clip was empty. She retreated from the edge of the ramp, out of range of a hail of bullets. She slapped the last clip into the Ingram.

Babette lay back from the ramp, waiting for the first head to appear above floor level. Her back was fanned by prop wash from the copter hovering overhead. She could not spare a second to look up; she could only hope it carried allies.

Screams—chilling, almost unreal—sounded. They were screams of fear, not agony. They were followed by a series of explosions. Bloodied bits of human beings rose, then fell. Babette risked taking a quick glance. She looked up at the copter from which the grenades had been lobbed into the attackers, but it was already landing at the entry to the parking building. She moved her eyes back to the ramps, determined to stop any survivors from surfacing.

Politician saw the two gunners from the car bringing their automatic rifles to bear on his partner. He fired on the run. The bullets stitched the car roof, nailing one of the gunners in the cheek, missing the other. Both of the bastards ducked low.

Gadgets forced them to duck even lower. Before the goons could think about getting off more shots, he fired a burst at one man's ankle and then the next man's. The guncocks crashed to the ground. Two more bursts guaranteed they would never get up.

Pol and Gadgets trotted back to the ramp to help Babette hold the fort. They could hear shooting from below.

Ten minutes later, following a two-minute silence, Carl Lyons called.

"Don't shoot. I'm coming up."

The men greeted each other.

Blancanales did the introductions. "Carl, meet Babette Pavlovski. Best backup gunner in the business."

They locked eyes. They locked hands.

"Nice to meet you."

HE WAS SIX FEET TALL with wide shoulders, a barrel chest, narrow hips. His white hair gave him the look of maturity; he did not look old. His complexion had a flushed, just-scrubbed appearance. His blue eyes carried little expression, but they had the ability to send chills through anyone who dared to stare into them. He talked to three young men who stood uncomfortably before him.

"There were how many of you?" he asked in a cold, clipped voice.

The three glanced around the room, each more than willing to allow the other to answer.

After several silent seconds, the eldest, a thirty-year-old still fighting a losing war against acne, answered. " 'Bout thirty-five of us went there."

"And only three of you survived?" The white-haired man's tone indicated that no amount of convincing would make him believe such a failure had occurred.

"Well. . . a couple of the guys may have surrendered," one of the Riding Devils confessed.

The third, still-silent member of the bikers was busy putting a small pinch of powder between his thumb and first finger. Then he inhaled the powder, snorting deeply.

"I suppose you were all enjoying the dust," the white-haired man said. "How much dust?"

"Not enough to get real high, Mr. Boering. Just enough to make sure no one got chicken shit."

"Just enough? Just enough. I want one goddamn woman taken care of... you send three Devil Riders...."

"Riding Devils," the sniffer corrected.

Klaus Boering ignored him. "I even supply the guns. But three is not enough to take care of one woman. So you send thirty-five and only three of you come back."

"She had two bodyguards. Then some sort of SWAT squad came," one of the bikers tried to explain.

"Oh," Boering sneered sarcastically. "Thirty-five of you went after one woman. Turns out she had two bodyguards. It was obviously a trap. How lucky you are to have escaped!"

The three shifted nervously, spending most of their time looking down at their feet, at the floor. They didn't know how to deal with Boering. The white-haired man was obviously furious over their inability to get the job done. He waved at them as if he were shooing chickens.

"Goodbye. Good-goddamn-bye. I have no more work for you. Get out. Close the door when you leave."

The three turned and shuffled out, too defeated to protest their treatment. As soon as they had left, Boering picked up the telephone and dialed.

"Georgi, this is Klaus. I want the special team

made operational immediately...I know they're for special use only. This *is* a special use.

"Listen. A small squad of one, two, three, maybe a couple more are protecting that damn defector. They just killed thirty or more goons to do it. The special team is the best. Use them. Take out Pavlovski and everyone around her.

"How's the other operation going? Are the athletes away clear? Good. If you hear from Frazer, give him my congratulations."

He signed off and hung up the telephone.

Soon he could forget about Pavlovski's bodyguards.

They would be dead.

He was sure of that.

7

"Welcome to my office," Carl Lyons said, laughing as his Able Team partners examined the trailer on campus.

"It's more spacious than Brognola's," Blancanales said. "How'd you swing this?"

"I phoned Archer, told him I wanted one of those portable offices used by construction companies and he got it. Magic."

"Presto. This is a bit better than the huts we're used to using in the jungles," Gadgets noted.

"How's the arm?" Politician asked Lyons. The blond warrior looked surprised. "I'd forgotten about it," he said with a shrug. Lyons never gave small pain anything more than small consideration.

The trio settled down on some heavy, scarred chairs.

"How long do you figure it'll take Babette to round up the black athletes?" Gadgets asked.

"They've got to come from other areas where they're staying," Pol said. "Unfortunately they're not all together. Doesn't really matter, though. We need the time for planning."

The three men outlined a plan, each pitching in

with suggestions, questions, until one solid block of strategy had been mapped out.

"I'm going to need squealers—miniature transmitters that send a constant signal—and tracking gear," Gadgets interjected at one point in the session.

"FBI or cops have them?" Lyons asked.

"Not exactly what I want," he replied, "but something close enough. I can modify them. I'll need some tuning crystals, too."

Lyons went to make a phone call. When he returned he told Schwarz, "They'll have what you need in a half hour. Be delivered here."

The discussion continued until there was a knock at the door of the trailer office. Babette Pavlovski let herself in. She was followed by eight blacks.

"That was quick," Gadgets said.

"We're quick," one of the athletes informed him.

The only athlete the members of Able Team recognized was Sam Jackson, the U.S. amateur heavyweight boxing champion. Jackson was a huge man with huge fists. The fists hung at his sides, lightly closed. Over the past few years he had earned the nickname "Lightning" for the fast way those fists burned, punished opponents.

"So you're Lighting Sam Jackson," Pol said. "You're supposed to have the quickest hands in boxing."

"What do you mean, 'supposed to'?"

Jackson moved close to Blancanales, shadow boxing, his fists a blur. The Able Team warriors were more than impressed.

"Yeah," fired Lyons to Pol. "What *do* you mean, 'supposed to'?"

Everyone sat down. Silence filled the room.

Lyons, not wanting to waste valuable time, broke the quiet.

"Babette tells us Old Lady Russia would embrace you people with open arms. What's the draw?"

"Babette should mind her own business," one of the athletes piped in.

"American athletes are my business," Babette said. "Since I defected—something that had nothing whatsoever to do with the Soviet Union—I have been hounded by Soviet scum. They feel my defection is a taint on communism."

Lyons broke in to repeat his question. "What's the draw?"

"There's no discrimination over there," a female athlete said.

"We'd be supported by the state," another said.

"We'd get better training," said another.

"Bullshit," said Lyons. "They're not luring you over there with a nickel-and-dime draw of no discrimination, state support, better training. Don't feed me that shit. I just ate. What's the draw?"

Again silence filled the room. The athletes looked at one another. Tension hung heavy. No one wanted to be the first to speak. Finally, Lightning Sam Jackson opened up.

"Draw's different for each of us," he said.

"What's being offered to Sam Jackson?" Blancanales asked.

Jackson looked pained. He was a man clearly more confident dodging punches than questions.

"Money, man. What else? Old Boering told me they'd get me money and I could keep my amateur status."

Once Jackson had opened up, the rest began to spill their stories, reluctantly at first, freely later.

When they seemed to have run out of steam, Pol told them about the kidnapping. He passed around the note he had found in the blond man's pocket. He urged them to keep the situation to themselves.

"Maybe Russia would be better," one athlete, shocked at the news of the kidnapping, said.

"That is Russia," Pol told them. "Those were Russian agents we killed at the airport. That's your sample of Russia. Kill, capture. . . ."

"No way," Jackson said as he finished reading the letter. "The Klan hates Commies. There's no way those bigoted bastards would help the Russians."

"They'd help the South Africans, though," Pol reminded him. "And how hard would it be to set them up for this? The South Africans could really benefit from recognition by the Olympic Committee, but not enough to make it worth the Klan's while to get involved this deep. More than the Klan's involved."

"What was the shooting around here all about?" Jackson asked.

Lyons gave it to them straight. "This morning three dudes from a local motorcycle gang walked into the women's gymnasium and shot at Babette. They killed Tracy Shaw."

That news brought the first strong emotional reaction from the group. That news hit home.

"We're telling the press that the gang members were shooting at each other and that a stray bullet caught Tracy," Lyons said. "I'll tell you that the gunmen were using weapons that are manufactured in East Germany and don't often reach the West. We're also telling the press that the same motorcycle gang, the Riding Devils, came here to finish the war that started this morning."

"And what are you telling us?" another athlete asked. "The truth, I hope."

"The entire gang rounded up any weapons it could find and came to finish the job on Babette. The FBI had planned to get a substitute Babette over here, but the real one arrived first. The bikers attacked her but they didn't succeed with anything other than getting themselves wiped out."

There were a few weak smiles around the room. Babette was well liked and highly respected among the athletes. When she had selected the ones she wanted present at the meeting, she had picked athletes who were leaders, who could sway other athletes' opinions if unity among the blacks was needed.

Knuckles rapped on the door. Two men carrying three attaché cases entered the room.

"Lyons?" one asked.

Lyons nodded.

The men placed the attaché cases on an empty desk. Lyons was required to sign a form, and then the men left.

Gadgets got up and seated himself at the desk. He opened the attaché cases. One case held tools, a second had two directional receivers, the third a large assortment of the squealers he had requested along with a batch of spare parts carefully mounted in foam rubber.

The Able Team wizard began dismantling the first small broadcasting unit.

"Any more questions?" Lyons asked the group.

"Yeah," one replied. "Why are you telling us all this?"

"I want something."

"That much we figured, but I'm beginning to suspect it's more than an oath of allegiance."

Lyons told them what he wanted. It took some time and discussion. While they batted ideas back and forth, clarifying points, Babette went over to help Gadgets.

One by one the black athletes agreed to the plan and left the stuffy trailer to walk in the late-afternoon sun.

When the last athlete was gone, Gadgets wiped the perspiration from his face and turned to Babette. "Where did you learn to solder like that?"

Sadness gripped her tone. "In Czechoslovakia, an athlete must start gymnastics so young. When I was nine I objected to such a strenuous life. I was always practicing or doing schoolwork. I never had time to play. I became bitter, and my performance dropped. Czech authorities knew I might act this way and they had a cure—putting me to work in a factory, twelve hours a day, six days a week. In the factory I soldered small electronic components. In the factory I learned to love the athletic life.

"It took me eleven months to be accepted back into the athletic program. When I was accepted, I became the hardest-working member of the gymnastics team."

Gadgets was held by her story; he was held because she was a fascinating woman. She could solder and soldier with the best, on top of coaching the U.S. team. She had placed her life on the line and yet she radiated warmth, a sense of humor, a love of life.

They stood looking at each other for seconds and would have remained that way if they had not been interrupted by a knock at the door. Gadgets was closest to the door. He opened it and was greeted by the grinning face of Petra Dix, the West Coast's famous face on television news.

8

"Yes?" Gadgets inquired.

"Jesus, you're a hard man to track down," Petra Dix said, her voice ringing as strong and clear as a cowbell.

"How did you manage it?" Gadgets asked, not budging from the doorway.

"Hey, come on. What's with the cold treatment? This is Petra Dix. We were rolling around on the ground together three hours ago. Don't pretend like you don't remember."

Lyons and Blancanales looked at each other and grinned. Babette glided over to the door to take a look at the brash-voiced creature who had the back of Gadgets's neck turning red.

"How could I ever forget," he said.

Dix wasn't quite sure how to take the comment. After a pause she said, "I want to thank you for saving my life."

"Any time."

"I also wanted to tell you that you're harder to fall on than pavement. Come on out here for a moment so I can thank you properly."

"I see you've got a cameraman waiting out there," Gadgets said. "I can't go out there, I'm shy as hell."

Dix laughed. "A man who makes a flying tackle at a lady in a public place can hardly go around calling himself shy. Come on."

Gadgets stayed indoors in the shadow of the doorway, carefully watching the cameraman. The video eye had not yet been trained on him.

Dix let out a huge sigh. Gadgets smiled. From his vantage point, he could understand and clearly see why the local joke about Petra Dix was: "The biggest thing she contributes to the news is cleavage." She made a sign of resignation then turned and spoke to her cameraman.

"Tony, put that damn thing down for a moment. Take a break."

Gadgets was about to step forward into the sunlight when a strong hand pulled him back. Before he could recover his balance, Babette had slipped out past him and was standing at the bottom of the trailer's metal steps. She surveyed the situation carefully. Petra Dix surveyed her.

Gadgets stood in the shadow watching the two women. Both were well built, but there the similarity ended. Babette's hair was cut short and had been brushed so that every hair was in place. Dix's hair was long and had a deliberately unkempt look. Her makeup, overdone for the television lights and cameras, looked wild. To Gadgets, she did not compare with Babette, who wore no makeup at all, preferring the natural look.

Petra wore an expensive, stylish suit. Babette wore jeans, sandals and a T-shirt. One woman was the product of careful packaging; the other was simply herself.

"What about the other cameramen you have in the van?" Babette asked Dix.

"I don't know what you're talking about," Dix replied, her voice controlled, and odd.

"Let's take a look then," Babette suggested.

She started across the small parking lot toward an unmarked blue van. The cameraman Dix had called Tony swung his scanner to his shoulder and started to follow her. Gadgets joined the procession, keeping Tony between himself and the van.

Just before Babette reached the van, the cameraman sprinted to one side to catch her profile. He crowded in closely as the gymnastics coach tugged at the handle on the van's rear doors. They were locked. She turned, the cameraman took a step closer and his camera flew from his hands. They all heard the boom of the heavy rifle that had fired the bullet.

Reactions were swift. Gadgets shoved the cameraman and Dix between the parked cars. "Get down and stay down," he yelled.

Babette scooped up the fallen piece of equipment and rammed it through one of the van's mirrored back windows. The broken window revealed a cameraman whose scanner had been thrust back into his eye.

"What the hell," the hidden cameraman exclaimed, trying to see who was responsible for the deep and dark shiner he was going to have.

Babette was already out of sight. She dodged around the side of the van, away from the sniper. A high-powered bullet, which had burst through one side of the van and out the other, whipped past her. She vaulted over two more cars, then ducked down.

Lyons and Politician had gone to the door to watch the confrontation between the two women. Neither had stepped outside. The crack of a high-powered rifle triggered them into action. There was a scramble for weapons.

Lyons thrust the M-203 at Pol, then pointed to two bandoliers containing clips for the M-16 part of the weapon and grenades to feed the M-79 part. Blancanales slung on two bandoliers and was gone.

Throwing open one of the wooden cases, Lyons grabbed a Champlin, already sighted in with a Kahles ZF69 scope.

Taking a box of the .458 Magnum shells in the other hand, he ran to the end of the trailer and used the rifle butt to take out a small windowpane. He quickly jacked a shell into the breech and knelt, using the scope to search the new building at the south end of the parking lot.

Gadgets was mad as hell—at himself. He was stuck in the open, armed with nothing but a Beretta and subsonic bullets. Compared to the big piece booming from one of the terraces on the new building, the Beretta was only able to dish out love taps.

"When all else fails," he muttered to himself, "attack." He took off in a weaving, choppy pattern, to cover the four hundred feet to the building where the sniper was at work. He knew the first leg of the run would be the most dangerous. As he drew closer to the edge of the building, the sniper would have a tougher shot. Gadgets ran like hell, breaking left or right with each few paces. A bullet dug asphalt two feet from his foot. He subconsciously braced himself for the next bullet.

Blancanales charged out with the M-203 in time to see his partner, hands empty, dashing for the sniper's base. He swerved to follow, searching his bandolier as he went. He found a smoke grenade and shoved it into firing position without slowing his run. Raising the M-203, he fired the grenade about fifty feet ahead of Gadgets. Again swerving hard and fast to make himself an elusive target, he reached for another smoker.

Petra Dix looked in disgust at the cameraman huddled on the floor of the van. The gaping holes in the side panels told her how close the bullet had come to hitting the man, but that did not matter to her. There was news to tape that took priority over everything. She reached inside the van and grabbed a portapak. She plucked the camera that was not damaged from the cameraman's hand and plugged it into the portable recording unit.

Keeping a hand over his sore eye, he looked up at her. "You can't use that," he said.

"Watch me," she replied.

She took off to catch the action.

Lyons found the sniper in his scope. By the direction the rifle was pointed, he guessed the gunner had Blancanales dead in his sights. He didn't wait for an exact shot. With the cross hairs on the assassin's forehead, he squeezed a quick shot. The 300-grain Magnum Super Speed plucked at the gunner's hair. The sniper's shot went wild.

Lyons quickly worked the bolt and with a fresh cartridge waiting to take up the argument, he continued to scan for the sniper. But the assassin had dropped out of sight. Lyons swept the terrace with the scope, determined to hold the sniper back from the edge.

When Gadgets saw the first ball of smoke, he veered so that the thick fog would be between himself and the sniper. Another "whump" sounded and smoke geysered up from the second grenade that Pol had launched. Gadgets swerved as if he planned on running behind this screen also. At the last second, he veered again, plunging into the smoke. The logical thing to do was make another sudden turn and emerge in an unexpected direction. But when you're being chased by bullets, you get into the mind of the enemy and outsmart them. He plunged straight ahead, taking the shortest possible route to the sniper's position.

Again the rifles ripped. The bullets were missing the mark and Gadgets was getting closer to his goal. On the dead run he realized there was more than one gunner. He was in a cross fire. Already he was at an awkward angle for the sniper and his backup posted on the new building. However, the gunner on the men's gymnasium had a clear field and was snapping a line of hot lead at Gadgets.

Lyons had one eye to the scope and the other open, giving himself a wider field of vision. He saw the muzzle-flash when the automatic rifle opened up. He swung the scope across. He was set to squeeze off his shot when his prey ducked to change clips. He swore and waited impatiently for the head to reappear. While he waited, Babette dashed into the trailer. As quickly as she came, she left.

When Babette had seen Petra Dix take off to get her news shots, she had decided it was as good a time as any to arm herself. She had made a mad sprint for the trailer, diving inside. No fire had been directed at her—Blancanales and Schwarz were taking the heat. Babette grabbed an Ingram, checking to make sure she had a full clip of regular ammunition. She also picked up two squealers fitted with strong magnets. Then she took off after Petra Dix.

She quickly caught up with the news reporter, who was in poor shape and was not used to running with twenty-five pounds of equipment. She halted the puffing reporter by reaching out, placing one hand on each side of the portapak's take-up chamber, and stopping.

"What the hell," Dix exclaimed.

"You're going to get yourself killed," Babette said.

"That's none of your goddamn business. I've got a story to cover."

Babette shrugged and let her go. She then started a weaving run, following Gadgets into the sniper's nest.

Pol saw the gunner on the roof of the men's gymnasium. He sent a burst of tumblers in that direction. The .223-caliber bullets came close enough to upend the rifleman. Pol veered, keeping the combo gun pointed toward the roof as he closed in.

The stairs were a killer, but Gadgets was not

about to risk the elevator. It was too easy for the bastards to have someone waiting to hose the cage as soon as the doors started to open. He knew he was up against top-notch pros.

The Able Team fighter's breath was coming hard, choppy. His calves, knees, thighs, were protesting the upstairs sprint. But he burst onto the large roof area without waiting to catch his breath. Every second was crucial. Every second could tell the difference between living and dying.

There was no one in sight. An old Stoner M63A1 lay near the edge of the roof. Beside it lay a couple of banana clips. Gadgets looked around, wary of a trap. There was nowhere for an ambusher to hide except inside one of the sealed windows.

Gadgets slowly walked backward, trying to watch all of the windows. The glass reflected sky. He could not see in. None of the windows had been broken. He reached the M63A1 and picked it up, keeping his eyes peeled on the building. The weapon was still warm.

Slipping the Beretta back into leather, he ejected the clip from the Stoner. It was empty. One of the other clips was also empty. The other was full.

It had been a skillful retreat. If Gadgets had found nothing on the roof, he would have rushed to overtake the gunman. With the weapon planted there, he had wasted valuable time sniffing for a trap. He slapped home the full clip and went to find the sniper's former position. He already had a damn good idea what he'd find there. He stared at the abandoned military model of the Remington

700, equipped with telescopic sight. He swore. The gunners had escaped. Alive.

Gadgets, sparked by a sound, turned quickly, and saw Babette covering him with an Ingram.

"Got away," he said in disgust. "The bastards got away. Thanks for the backup."

She nodded, but said nothing. Together they caught the elevator.

Gadgets and Babette walked out of the building. They were immediately confronted by the whirring camera toted by Petra Dix. Gadgets made a move to swing one of the weapons into the camera, but was stopped by Babette. He glared at her. She winked back.

Blancanales emerged from the men's gymnasium and Lyons from the trailer. The group converged in the parking-lot strip, not far from the van where the television cameraman was timidly peeking out.

"No one on the roof when I got there," Politician said, "but I found this." He held up a Stoner.

"Welcome to the club," Gadgets said. "I got the same."

"Hold the gun higher," Dix demanded.

The entire group turned toward the pushy reporter. Anger was apparent on their faces.

Lyons reacted with the anger he felt. He brought the Champlin up sharply. The rifle barrel knocked the lens from the camera. Dix dropped the camera.

"You son of a bitch," she screamed at Lyons.

Lyons ignored her screechy protests. His blue eyes fastened on her brown eyes. No tenderness passed between them.

"You were at the airport," Lyons fired, "and someone tried to shoot us. Now you show up here and we're shot at again. I want to know why."

Dix appeared more indignant than frightened. Gadgets saw her sneak a look at the portapak on her shoulder. Although the camera was smashed, everything she had recorded would still be on the tape in the heavy pack. Gadgets then noticed why Babette had stopped him from smashing the unit before, and he grinned.

"I have no idea who's trying to kill you," Dix retorted.

"No one said you did," Lyons said. "I'm just trying to put it in your pretty head that you're bad news. Bad luck. So why don't you pedal your ass out of here and stay away from now on."

"Who are you to tell me what to do?" Dix asked.

"I'm temporarily in charge of Olympic security," Lyons replied.

"And as his assistant," Pol said, "I'd like to know how you found us here in the first place."

Facing the head of Olympic security and his assistant—perhaps assistants—Petra Dix was losing a little bit of her practiced cool. She was beginning to think that pedaling herself out of there might be the best idea the security head had had. She surrendered a few trade secrets.

"We intercepted police broadcasts. We were too late to see any of the shooting, but when I saw the body count, I just figured you guys were around. We drove around campus until we finally found you. I, ah, I set up a little trap to get you on tape, but she spoiled it.'' Dix pointed an accusing finger at Babette.

Babette laughed. ''You must have forgotten that you used that same trick on me last year. Your act's wearing thin.''

Having heard her story, Lyons once again excused her from further action. ''You really should go now,'' he said. ''Beat it.''

Dix stole another look at the portapak hanging against her hip. Disdaining to pick up the broken camera, she climbed in beside the cameraman whom Gadgets had dumped between the two parked cars. The other cameraman was still crouched in the back of the van.

Babette walked over to the passenger side of the van and caught the door before Dix could slam it shut. She reached in and removed two objects from the side of the portapak.

''What are you doing?'' Dix snarled.

''I stored these there during the fight,'' Babette explained. ''We may need them again.''

''What are they?''

''Limpet mines. But it turns out we won't have to blow you up after all.'' Babette giggled at her own joke.

''Get me out of here,'' Dix demanded. ''They're all crazy.''

The driver needed no further encouragement. The cameraman in the back was warning Dix. ''Jesus, Petra, you're going to get us killed one of these days.''

"Shut up, wimp," Dix snarled. The door closed. They left rubber on the parking strip.

Lyons raised an eyebrow as Pavlovski returned, juggling two squealers.

"Those two transmitters are designed to be attached magnetically to a car," Gadgets explained. "Babette put the two strong magnets right by the tape storage on the recorder. I'm afraid the tape Petra Dix was so anxious to get out of here won't have a thing on it."

"Too damn bad," Blancanales said, unable to keep a straight face. "That's a heartbreaker."

When the laughter had subsided, Lyons told his partners that he was going to go to Edwards Base to arrange transportation and backup. "We've got to move on our plan," he said.

Lyons handed his rifle to Politician and headed for the car the FBI had left for him.

"I must get back to my team," Babette said.

Schwarz volunteered to go with her. He jogged over to the trailer to rid himself of excess weapons and to pick up a radio. He found the borrowed gym bag and loaded it before he set off.

Pol was left to guard the fort.

9

Klaus Boering knew he had the upper hand, but he was not enjoying it. The man in front of him was bumbling, verbally stumbling. He'd break any moment now. All of Boering's carefully laid groundwork was beginning to bear fruit. But something was making him feel uneasy. Very uneasy.

"You are finished in America," Boering told Zak Wilson, a lanky black eight-hundred-meter man. "When your stupid amateur committee finds what you've done with the money, you'll be banished from competition. Your name will be shit. You can take money, Zak, for wearing a particular running shoe—giving it your endorsement—but you have to put that money into a fund, put it away until your amateur days are over. You've spent it. And they're going to find out. That nosy reporter will find out, I know it."

Zak Wilson looked at Boering with contempt. Sure, he had accepted some cash. Most athletes do. Most put it in some hokey trust fund—a little cash pool that they can dive into when their athletic days have ended. But Zak had spent loads of his bread. He had wined, dined, bought antique cars, and spent and spent. Now this blackmailing bastard was threatening him, saying he'd take away Wilson's amateur status. If he lost that, he'd have nothing. He needed his amateur status to compete in the Olympics, which he planned to use as an international forum for his talent. Once his talent was exposed, he could cash in on it and retire.

Boering continued. "So why suffer? You'll be welcome in Russia or any Warsaw Pact nation you choose. We're not so silly there. We don't worry so much about amateur status. A little spending. We hide such petty crimes. In Russia you'll be treated with respect. With respect comes reward. Money."

Wilson shifted uneasily in his chair. He was thinking, churning the situation over and over in his head. Boering hadn't been a coach for twenty years without learning how to manipulate, push people.

When Boering had been activated for this project, he had thought it was a waste of a mole, a mole buried thirty years deep. He had made his mark on the West German swim team. Then, with the aid of the KGB, he had quickly moved into coaching. Using his pipeline with the Soviet Union, he had kept up to date on the Soviet's expertise in swimming and had become one of the most respected coaches in the NATO block. That was all the KGB controllers had ever asked of him—until now. Now he was to round up a group of black Americans and convince them to leave their country.

Once involved, it had taken Boering little time to understand the importance of the task he had been assigned. It was indeed worthy of a thirty-year mole. Couple his project with project "Klandestine" and all of Africa would fall in line with the Communist ideology.

Zak Wilson broke the silence.

"What do you want? What do you want from me?"

"I just want to help you, Zak. After the Games, why don't you join the other black athletes who are escaping the pettiness of this country. Why don't you come to where you are appreciated?"

"What other black athletes?" Wilson asked.

"You wouldn't want me slipping your name into conversations. Why would I mention other names?"

"There aren't any others."

"There are, but you'll have to take my word for it. I refuse to compromise anyone."

"Shit. Lay off that 'compromise anyone' crap. You don't think I know who tipped off that nosy reporter?"

"Really, Zak...."

"Save your bullshit and your 'reallys' for the suckers. How soon?"

"Immediately after the Games I'll arrange a scholarship for you. Then you can go to your new country, decide to stay—officially—and you'll have no trouble here before you leave."

"No trouble. What do you think I've got now? I've got damn Feds crawling all over me. I've got a reporter crawling all over me. After the Games is too damn late. Man, you're no use to me."

Zak Wilson, caught between a rock and a hard place, headed for the door. Boering waited until the angry runner was almost out before he spoke.

"I do have a couple of athletes leaving tonight. Can you be ready on time?"

"Tonight. Yeah. I can be ready."

"The University Elementary School at UCLA campus. North section where Sunset turns south. I'll be in the school parking lot at 7:30. I'll be in a large limo. Clear?"

"Clear. Anything else?"

"Bring only one small bag. Don't worry about what you leave behind. Everything you need will be provided."

"I'll be there."

"See you in two hours."

Zak slammed the door behind him.

Boering leaned back in the chair and stared at the door. No sense getting up to lock it, he thought. More sheep on the way. Boering, sitting in the lap of luxury in a hotel suite, could not shake that feeling that success, something that usually came with long, hard work, was coming a bit too quickly. Too easily.

A knock sounded on the door.

"Come in," Boering called. "It's not locked."

In walked Lighting Sam Jackson.

"Man," he gasped, a little out of breath. "I damn near bumped into Zak Wilson out there. I saw him getting into the elevator. I made it to the stairs before he saw me, but just barely."

"Zak was coming from here," Boering said with a smile.

Jackson relaxed visibly. "Zak Wilson. Zak Wilson is coming with us. What was his price?"

"Not everyone is as greedy as you are, Sam. Some people are moving to a socialist state strictly on principle."

"Yeah, right," he replied sarcastically as he rejected the offer of a chair, choosing the bed instead.

Jackson sat silent for a second, then asked: "You got it?"

"Of course, but I have a few questions."

"No questions this late in the game."

"Why now, Sam? Why leave now instead of after the Games? Why the others?"

"I've already told you."

"Tell me again."

Jackson sighed. "It's those Feds who came in after that gymnast was killed. They know the score and they know someone's been after the brothers to leave the country. They're dangerous dudes. I told you when I saw you earlier that anyone who was still going to go would want to go now before those guys get any closer to the truth."

"It seems you were correct. There will be a carload leaving this evening. It's too bad. After the Games would have made a lot greater impact, more of a show."

"Who's going tonight?" Jackson asked.

"You'll see when you get there. If I told you those trouble-makers will be taken care of, would you wait until after the Games?"

"Me personally, or all the athletes who are planning to desert the sinking ship?"

"Both or either."

"I doubt anyone would. I know I wouldn't. Anyone gets curious, it would be too easy to find out how many times you and I have talked. I think the others are crapping themselves even more than I am. Let's move this. I want to make a deposit into a bank here."

"You can always take it with you," Boering said. "Then you'll have the money in a place where you can get at it."

"I want the money now."

Boering steered the subject on to a new course.

"You think those Feds you're all running from will try to stop you tonight?"

"If they know what's coming down they will."

"Who would tell them?"

"Not me. Nobody. I don't think anyone has the nerve to tell those vultures anything. Whoever squeals will probably be taken into a quiet room somewhere and wrung out like an old undershirt. Mind you, I think they'll find out anyway. We're not dealing with turkeys."

"Then," Boering said, "one way or another, I'd better assure that we're not delayed."

Jackson stared at the ruddy-faced man. "You do what you have to. I still gotta get to the bank."

Boering reached behind his chair and produced a plastic shopping bag. He tossed it to Jackson. The boxer caught it and dumped the contents onto the bed. Stacks of fifty- and hundred-dollar bills littered the bed. Jackson started counting the bills in the bundles, his eyes aglow.

"You really don't have to go to all that trouble," Boering remarked, watching the boxer count the cash. "I'd be a fool to short you this late in the game."

"No trouble at all," Jackson said. "I've gone short so long, believe me, this is no trouble."

The counting was rapidly completed and the bundles tossed back into the bag.

COLONEL FRANK FOLLET CRUMPLED the piece of paper and threw it across the room. The tightly packed paper bounced off an aerial photograph of Edwards Air Force Base and came to rest between Victory's torch and wings. Victory was a piece of plastic mounted on a cheap stand. Follet had won the trophy in 1969 at the base's annual dart tournament. Colonel Frank Follet was as competitive as they come.

"Rat shit," the acting commanding officer of Edwards snarled. He said it to himself, having carefully waited until he was alone before throwing the paper—and a slight tantrum.

Twenty-one years of career service without attaining a command. Then, when General Bogart was sent to the European theater on only twenty-four hours' notice, Follet found himself not busily sewing stars on his uniforms, but merely being appointed acting CO. That stung. He had gone to his room in the officers' quarters and taken dart target practice on a photograph of the face of General Bogart. He had emerged from the room twenty minutes later ready to take over his temporary command.

But he had also emerged a determined man. He

had vowed he would show the idiots in the Pentagon that Bogart's failure to recommend Follet to replace him at Edwards was an act of spite—the act of a small mind unable to admit that his would-be replacement had a superior mind. He had vowed he would run Edwards so damn well anyone who was sent to the base as new commander would look like a jackass by comparison.

The first thing he had done as acting commander was double the fatigue duties. He wasn't out to win friends, he was out to win respect from high places. The lawns were cut twice as often, buildings that had not been painted for two or more years were given brand-new coats, inspections were doubled and the standards became more rigid. He would have the spiffiest base in the service or there would be hell to pay.

Then he had learned about the Soviet trawler. One of the lieutenants on radar duty had been glancing at a scope that was really a monitor of a scope operated by the Coast Guard. Questioned by Follet, the young lieutenant had reported that the image was that of a Soviet trawler. It was just outside the U.S. territorial limit and was being monitored from the radar on a small ship that was tagging the Russian vessel. The image was then bounced comsat to all military bases in the area.

It had not taken Colonel Follet long to realize that this was a golden opportunity to flex his muscles and impress some people. The trawler, according to all concerned, was probably a spy ship. Follet deduced that if it in fact was a spy ship, it was probably carrying a helicopter. And when that chopper went on its mission, the man who planned the interception would be lauded. Follet reasoned that if the other bases were paying as little attention to their monitors as the Edwards base had been, it would be easy for him to steal the show. He assigned a man to watch the monitor.

He was feeling quite pleased with himself, but then the memo came from Washington. It said that some Washington pimp had been put in charge of national security. It said that because of potentially explosive problems at the Olympic Games, this Washington pimp needed—and was to be given— full cooperation. It was signed by the President of the United States.

Follet had crumpled the note up and tossed it, but now he picked it back up. Again he swore.

The telephone rang. He snatched it up and growled into it.

It was the secretary to the base commander.

"The gate is on the line, sir. They have an unidentified male who claims to have presidential authority. He's got some sort of crumpled-up document that looks authentic. He's asking for you."

Follet was tempted to order the nut locked up. But he would never get near a command if he did that to political errand boys. He had played politics for twenty-one years; he knew how the system operated.

"Have him escorted to my office," Follet said finally.

A jeep loaded with MPs screeched up to escort Carl Lyons to the base commander's office.

"Go right in, sir," the secretary said after Lyons had been dropped off. "Colonel Follet's expecting you."

The royal treatment was a bit much for Lyons. Such plastic respect did not give him a good feeling. It made him gag.

He entered the colonel's office. Follet, six foot three, lean, came striding around the desk with his hand thrust forward.

"Glad to meet you, sir," the colonel said, squeezing lies between his teeth. "I'm Colonel Follet. Come to assume command?" he asked. His voice was pitched high and weighted with a tone that was too eager to please.

Lyons supplied his name, then said, "Listen, I don't know what you're talking about. I'm not interested in taking over. But I do need some close cooperation."

"Anything at all, Mr. Lyons. Name it."

Lyons sat down without being offered a chair. Follet frowned at the breach of etiquette. Lyons bit his lip.

"I need your fastest helicopter—one that can take three passengers and gear—on standby at the UCLA campus."

Follet, now sitting behind the large desk, continued to frown. "I'm afraid we can't do that," he said. "Landing inside city limits other than at specific helipads isn't done except in an emergency."

"This is an emergency," Lyons said. "Have it ready to take off in ten minutes. I'll go back to town in it."

"Then you're taking full responsibility?"

"Yes," Lyons said, his voice tough as iron. Lyons had no trouble conjuring up a look of menace. The Able Team warrior was a menacing man.

"No trouble then," the colonel said. "Anything else?"

"I want a troop of Marines on standby at Twenty-nine Palms. I want you to phone the CO at that base and confirm my identity. That'll save me time."

Follet's jaw clenched, yet he managed to force a small frozen smile onto his face. Lyons had to grin—the colonel's face looked like it was going to crack.

He made the call Lyons had requested.

"I trust that takes care of things."

"The helicopter," Lyons impatiently reminded him.

"Oh, yes. Of course." Follet put through the orders.

By the time he had hung up the telephone, Lyons was on his feet. "The car I drove here," he instructed. "Have it returned to the small parking strip near the women's gym at UCLA."

He was out the door. When the door slammed shut, Follet let the smile drop from his face. He reached into his desk and pulled out a fistful of darts. Slowly, with all the power his arm could produce, he drove each dart into the door.

10

Ellie Kay King had no trouble finding her friend, Mustav Zubimi. He was occupying a double seat on the school bus. When he saw Ellie he smiled. It had been a long time apart for two close friends.

"Kelly," he exclaimed, "so good to see you." His English was textbook perfect.

Kelly looked around, hoping none of the "guides" had heard the 290-pound weight lifter's warm welcome. With all the commotion outside the vehicle, none had noticed.

"Shhh. Move over," she whispered.

The iron pumper moved his large frame as close to the window as he could squeeze.

"Barely have room for you," he said. "And you're so skinny."

Kelly wedged herself onto the small space Zubimi had left her.

"What are you doing here?" he asked her.

Before Kelly could reply, gunfire sounded outside the bus. The last Zambian athlete was literally thrown on the bus. The bus was already in reverse when the last two "guides" clambered on board. The vehicle lurched forward and the whites distributed themselves up and down the aisle, guns in their hands.

Kelly wrapped her arms around Mustav and pulled herself up to his ear. She whispered. "Tell your teammates not to speak English. Tell them to pretend they know no English. We're being kidnapped. No time to explain."

Mustav, keeping his features calm, smiled and asked no questions. He leaned forward and whispered in one of his teammate's ears. Then he turned and whispered to a teammate sitting behind him. The word spread, Zambian athletes whispering instructions.

As the bus roared away from the parking lot, one of the guards spoke to an athlete. "What the hell are you doing? What's with this whispering?"

The athlete started talking a blue streak—in his native tongue.

"Sweet shit," the white muttered to himself. He pushed between two whispering athletes, hoping that he could communicate his wishes through violence.

As the bus ride continued, the guards began to relax and talk more freely. They openly insulted the athletes, believing the blacks could not understand a word they were saying. And they talked of their plans. In little time the Zambians knew they had been kidnapped by the Ku Klux Klan. Though fear gripped their well-tuned bodies, they kept a calm mask covering their features.

The kidnappers drove their catch through Lancaster, along Highway 14, until it ran into Highway 395. At one point, the vehicle's CB radio crackled on and the bus turned on to back roads for about twenty miles. Eventually it went back to 395 and continued on its course.

"We seem to be heading for Death Valley," Kelly quietly said to Mustav.

"I won't tell the others," he replied. "They may take offence at the name."

An hour later, they went through Townes Pass and began the steep descent into the desert. The brakes on the ancient school bus caused almost as much fear as the kidnapping itself.

Finally the bus came to a creaking halt in the desert, and the guides forced the athletes off. The blacks were handcuffed into the passenger seats of dune buggies. Soon the bus was on its way again, empty save for the driver.

The fleet of brightly painted dune buggies took off north across the rolling, windblown sand. The group looked like one of the area's many buggy clubs having an outing. But one thing set the convoy apart from normal club outings: trailing the group were three vehicles carrying large propellers. The whirling props obliterated all tracks.

Kelly tried to keep some kind of idea of the distance of their journey, but the changes in speed and the rolling sand made it impossible. In less than half an hour the cavalcade of dune buggies had made the trip and had arrived at a camp.

The young gymnast could hardly believe what she saw. Between two dunes was stretched a large piece of netting, supported by pipe that had been driven into the sand at a sixty-degree angle away from the netting. Ropes and stakes kept each piece of pipe from shifting forward. Accordions of barbed wire stretched around the pipe supports. The netting had bits of sand-colored material attached at irregular intervals. It yielded quite a bit of shade to the encampment beneath.

Someone from inside had already swung open a cattle gate that was also festooned with the dangerous, flesh-shredding wire. The dune buggies entered in single file, passing two alert guards holding submachine guns.

The inside of the compound had a large parking area. There were several tents. But what really caught the eyes of the athletes were the patio tables with brown umbrellas and sandbags for chairs, which were placed regularly around the perimeter.

The dune buggies stopped inside the gate. The prisoners in them were freed and motioned to stand in a cleared area. The buggies were then parked side by side in the parking area.

When Mustav was freed, he went to stand near Kelly. He nodded toward the patio tables and then leaned down and whispered. "Look at the crazy guard posts."

"Shut up," a nearby guard spat.

Kelly and Mustav turned to face the guard, puzzled looks on their faces. Mustav began to talk in his native tongue.

"Speak English," the Klansman guard replied.

Most of the captors were middle-aged and potbellied. Two or three younger, fitter men were among them. One of the lean, younger ones spoke up. His drawl was overwhelming.

"Shit, Ned. English is their national language. They're pulling your leg." Leg became a three-syllable word.

Ned, angered at being made a fool of, glared at Kelly. "Maybe you'd like a little rifle-butt massage?"

"Jerk," Kelly snarled.

The enraged Ned swung the rifle butt at her head. A huge black hand plucked the M-16 out of midair, then twisted it out of the grip of the guard. Before anyone could react, Mustav, still holding the weapon by the barrel, passed it to another guard. The stunned guard accepted it. The weapons that were pointed at Kelly and Mustav relaxed.

"Take it easy, Ned," a young, hard-looking Klansman instructed. "We want them alive and unharmed if possible. If one of them gets too lippy, use the sandbags."

Ned wasn't about to take it easy; his pride was bruised. He made a move toward the mountainous Mustav. Kelly's foot shot out. The Klansman felt his testicles being driven hard into his guts. He fell in a moaning heap.

Again the guns went up.

The young Klansman took charge. He ordered the guards to move the captives out of the baking sun and into one of the two large tents.

As the athletes were being placed in their pen, one of the hardmen took care of Ned.

"Shoot the silly shit full of morphine and put him to bed. He's no use to us like this," another of the young men said. The other guard dragged the moaning man through the sand to a tent on the far side of the parking area.

The athletes all lay flat on the sand floor of the tent. The floor was dug four feet into the ground, below the desert surface, and was much cooler than outside.

From their travels with the talkative guards they knew they were being held until the Klansman received one concession from the Olympic Committee. Then, supposedly, they would be returned. Somehow the athletes doubted this part of the plan.

"Well," Mustav mumbled, "what have you got up your sleeve, Kelly?"

"I went to the airport with an FBI man," she said, "and met three of the toughest guys I've ever seen. They were in that gunfight that caused our quick exit. They know we're gone. I'm not saying they'll find us for sure, but they're our best bet. Until they get here we obviously have to take care of ourselves."

"What were you doing with Feds?" Mustav asked.

Kelly's eyes misted over.

"I was at the gym training when these guys— these hoods—came in and tried to shoot Babette. They tried to kill Babette because she's a defector, I guess. They hit. . .they killed Tracy Shaw. Babette got away."

"Holy," Mustav muttered. "These guys are really playing for keeps."

"Mustav," another athlete said. "Why didn't you do something when you had that man's gun?"

"We'd have been slaughtered," Kelly answered for him. "He should have just let me pay the price for baiting that idiot."

"What happens if your men don't find us?" someone questioned.

"We take them out when they least expect it," Mustav answered. "We must prepare, plan together. No more back talk, no resistance. We have to help them relax."

"There's three of them out there that really scare me," a female athlete said.

"I know which three," Kelly said. "They're younger, harder looking. We'll have to be extra careful around them."

"The rest of them seem as nervous as we are," Mustav said.

"Let's soothe them," Kelly instructed. "Scared people are the dangerous ones."

The group agreed then lapsed into silence.

11

Sam Jackson was the last man to arrive at the school parking lot. He was swinging a small flight bag and swaggering. Lightning Sam Jackson was proud of himself; he had dramatically changed his economic standing. By selling out he had moved up in a world he believed conspired to keep him down.

"You're late," Boering snapped.

But the KGB mole did not look at Jackson. Instead, his eyes were fixed on a man who had been following the large boxer.

Jackson grinned at the mole. "I knew you wouldn't leave without me. I'm prepaid."

He slung his flight bag into the open trunk.

"Who's that behind you?" Boering asked.

"Damned if I know. Some wino who asked me for a buck."

The wino was a squat, roly-poly man whose body looked and smelled as though it had not benefited from a bar of soap or a razor in days. He was wearing an old suit that was a good tailor away from a good fit: in some places it was short, in others it was long. The wino was about to accost the boxer again. Boering stepped forward and the derelict veered toward him.

"Can you give me a buck for a bowl of soup?" the wino slurred. "I haven't had anything to eat all day."

Jackson stepped in front of Boering and gave the pudgy drunk a shove. "Beat it," he said, his voice dripping with contempt.

The wino staggered back a few steps and swayed. He looked at the boxer with loathing.

"No nigger treats me like that," he screamed. And then he charged. Fists flailing like windmills, the wino was inches from Jackson when the lightning-quick boxer showed off his reflexes, stepping easily to one side. The attacker went headfirst into the trunk of the car. Jackson laughed and grabbed the man's legs, stuffing the rest of his body into the trunk. He slammed the cover.

"What did you do that for?" Boering snarled.

"I couldn't hit the little shit," Jackson replied. "I'd have killed him."

Boering fished the car keys out of his pocket and unlocked the trunk. Jackson reached in, grabbed and lifted the drunk and deposited him on the ground. The wino curled up in a ball and began sobbing. Jackson gave a short snort of disgust and walked to the limousine, climbing into the front seat. Four of his teammates, three in the back and Zak Wilson in the front, were already in the car.

"Greetings, fellow traitors," he said as he hopped in.

No one answered.

Boering climbed in and started the car. The air conditioner blasted out a stream of cold air. Jackson, Wilson and another athlete looked back as the car pulled away. The lone figure still lay huddled on the parking lot.

Boering drove toward the San Diego Freeway. After covering two blocks he pulled over to the curb and stopped the car. He reached across his passengers and removed what looked like a cheap transistor radio with a short antenna from the glove compartment.

"What's that?" Jackson asked.

"A precaution," Boering replied.

Boering told the athletes to step out on the sidewalk. He approached them with the gadget and carefully scanned them, pointing the antenna at all parts of their bodies.

He came up empty. The KGB agent then turned his attention to the car. When he reached the back of the car, the instrument began to squeal. It took him only ten seconds to find the transmitter. It was fastened magnetically under the bumper. He removed it and opened the trunk. There were no squeals from the baggage or the inside walls of the trunk. However, a quick exploration under the car revealed another transmitter near the back of the vehicle.

"Those CIA types are stupid," Boering spat. "Your drunken friend left us one easy bug to find and then a hard one to find. Did he really think I'd be so stupid as to stop looking when I found the first?"

Cars were stopped nearby for a traffic light. Boering jogged over to one of the vehicles and attached the bugs.

When he returned, Jackson stepped in front of him.

"Wasn't my friend," he said.

"Are you sure?" Boering asked, looking almost amused.

"I'm sure."

Boering poked the transmission detector inside the car and probed around. There was no response. He straightened and retracted the short aerial. He put the device back in the glove compartment as the athletes got back into the car. The KGB man pulled the car back into traffic and onto the approach to the San Diego Freeway.

"Jackson," he said, taking his eyes off the road for a second. "I'm glad he wasn't a friend of yours. He's dead."

HERMANN GADGETS SCHWARZ WAS LYING on the asphalt of the school parking lot as the limousine disappeared from sight. Suddenly he heard three noises—the high-powered distant crack of a rifle, the lower-powered crack of a nearby gun, and the whip-snapping sound of a bullet tearing past his ear.

He didn't wait for other sounds. Rolling to his feet, he took off in a weaving run, hoping to make it to the wall of the nearest building.

There were two more cracks, one distant, one close. A bullet hit the tarmac by Gadgets's feet. It seemed to come from the building he was running toward, but there was no time to change direction. He moved faster, cursing the awkward clothing and padding he wore.

There was another distant rifle sound. No bullet came near Schwarz. He nipped around the edge of the building, cutting himself off from the other school buildings. He glanced up to see if a gun was poking over the edge of the roof. None, so far. Bringing his eyes down, he caught a flash of light from the parking lot between the school buildings and Sunset Boulevard. He threw himself flat just as a string of slugs chewed up brick and glass where he had been standing. Gadgets was thankful for the fool who had put an optic on the submachine gun. The flash from the evening sun had barely given him enough warning.

The distant gun boomed twice more. Gadgets was on his feet and running again to put a building corner between himself and the parking lot. As he ran, he tried to get under the padding to draw his Beretta.

The goon in the parking lot must have emptied his clip. The gun did not start barking again until Gadgets was nearly at the corner. As he pulled around the corner, brick chips stung one ear. He ran full tilt into a KGB executioner.

The guy was wearing a camouflage-green skin-tight combat suit. He had a bandolier of clips thrown over one shoulder and a quick-release rig. He was holding a Makarov on the other shoulder. In his hands he carried a Kalashnikov AKS74, fitted with a scope.

Gadgets did not even have time to bring his hand out from under the padding. He swung his elbow, connecting solidly with the gunner's windpipe. As the man went down, Gadgets drove his left hand into the goon's jaw. There was a snap, loud and brutal. The man carrying the Communist weapons was dead before he hit the ground.

Gadgets forgot about digging out the Beretta. He hastily tore off the tramp clothes and padding. His own clothes were underneath. He was grateful for the flak jacket's cooling system; without it he would have fried. He threw the bandolier over a shoulder, slipped the Makarov into one of the pockets in his pants and picked up the Kalashnikov. He checked the weapon's magazine, then took off around the corner of the building.

The Able Team member could hear the welcome booming of a Champlin, operated by Blancanales from the top story of the parking garage where they had held off an entire motorcycle gang earlier in the day.

Hitting the pavement, Gadgets brought his head around the corner of the building from a prone position. He hoped to spot the gunners—before the bastards spotted him. A bullet burned air inches from his nose. He'd been spotted. The gunner on the roof of the other school building had wedged himself between the air-conditioner box and the roof of the building, leaving Politician squat to shoot at.

The wing of the building holding the Russian sniper stretched well past the building that was sheltering Schwarz. Trusting his buddy to hold the man pinned, Gadgets retreated. When he had pulled back one hundred feet, he made a dash for the end of the wing of the building sheltering the sniper. It was a gutsy move that paid off. Schwarz made it to the wall before the gunner even got a shot off.

Keeping as close to the wall as possible, Gadgets moved until he found a maintenance ladder leaning against the side of the building, away from the parking lot. As he went up the ladder, he heard the Champlin speak twice, its retorts keeping the KGB killer pinned.

Gadgets crouch-walked to the far side of the air-conditioner housing. The Champlin sounded three more times, but the bullets were missing the mark. Pol seemed to be having difficulty keeping the third member of the KGB hit team pinned down. Gadgets decided to creep over the top of the housing. When he eased his head up, he almost lost it. A rapid burst of fire from the corner of the other school building clanged off metal. He jerked back.

He pulled the Makarov from his pocket and tossed it over the housing. The KGB killer's taut nerves reacted to the flying, dark object as if it were a grenade. The highly trained specialist flipped himself around the housing in a fraction of a second—right into a stream of 5.45mm slugs fired by Gadgets, who had taken off on the run as soon as he tossed the Makarov. The gunner's face was turned into a bloody, shredded mess.

The next logical thing to do was to throw himself flat, out of the line of fire of the remaining KGB guncocks. But the Able Team fighter was not feeling logical. Lyons wasn't around to be hard-assed and unpredictable, so Gadgets took over. He kept running straight at the Kalashnikov AKS74 barrel that was swinging to bear on him from the corner of the other building. He ran straight off the edge of the building.

Letting gravity grip him and drop him down, Gadgets fired the rest of the clip toward the building, aiming just above the submachine-gun barrel. Two of his bullets chewed at a piece of arm.

Gadgets landed easily from the ten-foot drop, rolling to his left as soon as he touched down.

Knowing that his target was down and rolling, the wounded KGB killer took two seconds to change clips, then charged around the corner, finger tightening on the trigger of the submachine gun. His steps suddenly turned into a rubber-legged stagger as his right arm and left leg exploded, sending pieces of flesh and bone airborne. The scum's face slammed into a brick wall, changing the features from ugly to uglier. Gadgets had heard the rumbling sounds of Politician's big Champlin and he knew that once again he owed his life to a fellow member of Able Team.

Politician had seen the attack coming and he had prepared himself for three quick, well-placed shots. His aim was deadly.

Gadgets scrambled to his feet and walked over to examine the last opponent, now lying dead in a puddle of blood. Gadgets searched for intel into the ambushers. He tore open the camo fatigues. Underneath was battle armor that look like Kevlar. It had done little to discourage the entry of a 500-grain avenger. He rolled the corpse over. It was little consolation to the wearer, but the jacket had prevented the spent slug and gore from exiting.

Gadgets looked at the face from quarter view. It was disturbingly familiar. Puzzled, he walked to the man he had killed with his hands. That face was not familiar. He started for the ladder to the roof of the other building and met Pol on the way.

"Thanks," he said. "I owe you one."

Pol shrugged off his friend's talk. "Think you'd do the same for me."

The pair stepped around the air-conditioner housing and rolled the body onto its back. The soft cap came off. Long, blond hair spilled out.

"A woman," Pol said.

"A bitch," Gadgets muttered.

The two men quit the battlefield.

12

Alf Inkster had a nervous, tight feeling in his guts. He did not really know why, but Captain Young always made him feel that way. Inkster looked again at the flight plan Young was filing. He wished he had his air controller, who understood these things, but the man had recently quit.

"You're doing a night jump over the Mojave Desert?" Inkster asked.

Captain Young just nodded. The lanky pilot was not one to waste words.

"Long way to go for a desert when there's plenty right around here," Inkster ventured.

Again Young nodded. Inkster waited for an explanation, but the captain supplied none. Inkster knew the man was cleared for night work; he had watched him acquire his licenses right here at this small airport.

When the airport had lost its only controller, Inkster had been sure they would have to close. He could not possibly bid for a new man in the competitive market and when he tried to direct air traffic, he grew dangerously confused. Fortunately, Captain Young and the Southern Survivalist Parachute Club had vowed to remain. On the few occasions when the airport had several planes to handle at once, Young or one of the other pilots from the SSPC took control of the radio and organized things.

"Guess it's not such a farfetched idea," Inkster picked up lamely. "You got a copy of the weather report?"

Young had.

"Good flight."

Young left.

Alf Inkster watched him walk across the tarmac. It was ninety-two sweltering degrees outside. Just the thought of ninety-two degrees made Inkster sweat, even though he was being cooled down by air conditioning. He shook his head. That Young was a cool bastard. Young went into the cinder-block SSPC house at the corner of the airport. Permission to build the clubhouse had been granted only because it meant the little airport could stave off bankruptcy. Inkster had never set foot inside the building, and he had no desire to. The Survivalists gave him the creeps.

Inside, Peter, the club's other pilot, was poring over maps and charts. Everyone else was checking weapons.

Young walked over to a large map of southwestern United States. He picked up a pool cue, which he used as a pointer. He slapped the cue against the wall, gaining everyone's attention. The club members fell silent.

"We'll be jumping at the crack of dawn," Young began.

"Wouldn't it be safer if we hit them in the dark?" one of the men said.

"No," Young replied. "We'll be going down while it's still dark, but it'll be easier if we have just enough light to tell friend from enemy. Don't forget there's three of our men in that camp. We want to get them, and only them, out alive. We have to wait until the desert is as cool as it's going to get in order to pinpoint the hidden camp with the infrared scanner.

"Now, pay attention," Young continued. "We want a complete wipeout of the blacks and the Klansmen. But we've got to keep those dune buggies in shape because that's how we're getting out of there."

"I'd rather be using a good machine pistol or a sawed-off shotgun than these M-16s," another club member complained.

Young turned and looked straight into the eyes of the speaker, giving the man a gaze so cold it forced him to shiver.

"You'll use only the assigned arms. You'll be inspected before boarding the DC-3. No one carries a favorite weapon. You have the same weapons that are issued to the U.S. Marines. One of the armed forces is going to be blamed for this massacre. It's going to look as if the United States fumbled again in trying to free the hostages. They'll deny it, but who will believe them? No one. So, taking anything into the battle zone that isn't consistent with that story will get you killed—by me. Is that clear enough?"

All agreed. It was crystal clear.

KLAUS BOERING WAS WITHIN SIGHT of Edwards Air Force Base. He constantly kept watch in his rearview mirror, checking for possible tails.

Helen, a cynic and the only female athlete in the limousine, questioned the driver.

"Boering," she said, "what the hell's coming down? We're heading toward Death Valley. You're supposed to be taking us out of the country, not deeper into it."

"I'm taking you to a temporary camp until I can get a helicopter to pick you up later tonight," the mole answered.

"Terrific," Helen said, not sounding convinced.

GADGETS, POL, BABETTE AND TWO BODYGUARDS sat in the trailer / office listening to Lyons squawk at them through the small radio speaker.

"How do we get to where the action is?" Pol asked Lyons.

"I'll have the base send another chopper. You may as well stand by until we see where our bird's going to nest.

"By the way, Gadgets, he must have done a second scan for bugs. All transmission stopped for twelve minutes."

Gadgets laughed. "I told you, nothing's more reliable than a simple on/off switch. We'll watch for the chopper and one of us will stand by the radio. How's your fuel?"

"This is a long-distance mother. Pilot tells me we have four hours left. We're less than half an hour from bases we can use."

"Okay. If the car doesn't stop in two hours, I'll take out the chopper you're sending and you can nurse the radio," Gadgets answered.

"Right. Sign off."

Gadgets turned his attention to Babette. "You'd better get some sleep. This could go on all night."

"You look like you need rest more than I do," she countered.

"Yeah," Gadgets admitted, stifling a yawn. "It's been a helluva long day."

"Why don't you take Babette home?" Pol suggested. "Then find a place to crash. Take your communicator and I'll buzz you when something happens."

"What about you?" Gadgets asked.

"I caught some sleep before this came down. You're the one who spent half the night screwing around with those electronic thingeys."

"Thingeys," Gadgets repeated, laughing.

"I don't know what they're called," Pol said in mock anger, not in the least apologetic about his ignorance of electronics.

"You sure don't," Gadgets replied.

Then he got up. "Come on, Babette. I'll take you home."

When she rose to go to the door, two newly assigned bodyguards also stood up.

"Wait a moment," one said. "I'll check outside."

Gadgets picked up the gym bag he had been using and rechecked its contents. He had added a few items. He slung the strap over his left shoulder. He left the zipper open.

"Coast is clear," the bodyguard said.

The other guard opened his suit jacket and checked the spring clip on the Ingram that rode harnessed to his left side. He then went out, glanced about and nodded to Babette to follow.

The trailer was in the parking lot on the west side of the women's gymnasium. The trailer door faced west. As they stepped out, the low sun shone in their eyes. The two guards were standing at the foot of the metal steps.

"Let's walk," Babette suggested.

"Okay," Gadgets said. Although his guts told him it was a bad move, his heart told him that the gutsy woman needed to go on with her life—not be caged in by fear of bullets.

One bodyguard hastened to move to point, the other paused to fall in behind. They started to move around the trailer and head east. As soon as they were facing that way, two hollow gunshots sounded behind them.

Gadgets shoved Babette forward with his right hand. With his left he yanked the Ingram from the bag.

"Cover her," he commanded.

With the Ingram questing a target, he ran back toward the few remaining parked cars. He ran directly into a blinding flash of light.

"Don't shoot, for chrissakes," a voice bellowed at the top of its female lungs. "You'll kill me."

Gadgets pulled himself short and went into a combat crouch, waiting for his vision to clear. As the black spots shrank he could make out the woman who owned the voice.

It was Petra Dix.

An electronic flash unit softly recycled. Lying on the roof of the car was a starter's pistol, which Dix had used to get Gadgets to face her camera lens.

The camera flashed again.

Gadgets let out an angry roar and leaped to the hood of the car, swinging his gun barrel at the offending camera. But Dix was expecting the attack. She snatched the camera out of his reach. She turned and ran toward a car farther down the row. The door was open and the motor running.

Gadgets moved from car hood to car hood, hoping to cut her off. When Dix reached her car, the door was slammed in front of her. Babette stood by the door. Her two bodyguards, faces flushed from trying to keep up, were behind her.

Babette plucked the camera from Dix's hand, using her quick reflexes. The gymnastics coach placed the camera on the roof of the car and began advancing on the reporter, who was backing away.

"You can't do this. It's harassment. I'm the press," Petra puffed.

"Harassment," Babette scoffed. "You've been trailing this man like a regular tracker and I want to know why."

"He's in a public place. I have a right to photograph—"

"Of course you do," Babette interrupted. "But with someone shooting at us—and you in the cross fire—your camera might have been hit or you could have dropped it."

"I wouldn't have dropped the camera," Dix shouted. "There was no shooting."

"No shooting," Babette mocked. "I could have sworn I heard shots."

"I just wanted a picture," the newswoman growled. "This man is part of some hit squad working for the government. The people have a right—"

While Babette was talking, Gadgets was bringing the Ingram up. His first burst shut the woman up and knocked her camera to the ground. The next burst cut the lens from the mount. The burst that followed swept the pieces across the parking lot.

"Looks like your camera got caught in the cross fire," Gadgets said. "Hate to have to tell you what I think about your hunch about some sort of government hit squad."

Dix looked at the camera then at the stony faces around her. In a fury she climbed into her car and burned rubber out of the parking lot.

One of the bodyguards spoke up. "Uhh, maybe we could take a car."

"Next time maybe you guys could do a little better search before we come out," Gadgets said.

The foursome went to get a car.

"It's your shot, Colonel."

Follet eyed the dart board. His score was sixty. A double twenty would finish the game. For Follet it was a relatively easy shot to make. He drew back his arm.

"Colonel Follet, you're wanted in communications."

He was too late to stop his shot. The dart missed the entire board, landing with a dull thud in the wall paneling. The twenty officers in the officers' club finished their drinks in eager anticipation of having a free one on Follet—that being the penalty for hitting the wall.

Follet stared at the second lieutenant who had interrupted his shot. The young man had the feeling he would be drawing garbage jobs for the rest of his hitch. The officers were already collecting their free drinks, which would automatically go on Follet's bar tab. Without saying a word, the grim-faced acting commander headed for the communications room.

· "Hate to be the poor bastard responsible for that message," one major murmured to another. "Old Folly'll try to ram him up the ass with a poison dart."

Lyons talked to the pilot as he waited for Follet to come to the radio. "The way that signal is headed, how long would it take us to refuel and get back to where we could pick it up again?"

"There's all sorts of places where we can refuel in an emergency, sir. I doubt if we'd lose the signal for more than twenty, thirty minutes."

Lyons had a few seconds to think before an angry Follet got on the radio.

"Acting Commander Follet here," he snapped.

"Lyons here. We need another long-range copter. Send it to UCLA right away."

"But that's impossible," Follet protested, some of the anger having dropped from his voice. "We only have two of the H-76s with the extra tanks."

"That's fine. Send the other to UCLA. Now.

Have it land at the women's gymnasium building. Make it fast. It may have to come and relieve me while we refuel.''

"I'll send a light Hughes for the job. Saves fuel, plenty fast enough for local jumps."

"You'll send an H-76, Colonel."

"Ahhh," Follet said, realizing the futility of arguing with the Able Team member, "yes, sir."

"The Marine company standing by?"

"Yes, sir."

"You got a larger transport chopper standing by in case the two Sikorskys aren't enough?"

"As of right now I do, sir," Follet said grudgingly.

"Good, Colonel," Lyons said. "Over and out."

GADGETS SCHWARZ YAWNED DEEPLY on his way up to Babette's apartment. The small elevator was crowded with the two FBI guards. A third guard had remained with the car; his duty was to watch the front of the building.

One of the bodyguards took Babette's key and went through her apartment before letting anyone else enter. The other man proceeded to the roof to take a position overlooking the fire escape. When the agent was finished checking the apartment, he motioned for Gadgets and Babette to enter, then took up a post guarding the door.

Once inside, Gadgets wandered around the apartment, looking through doors, locating the fire escape, glancing out at buildings that could possibly house a sniper.

"Don't you trust the man who just searched the place?" Babette asked.

"I stay alive by not totally trusting anyone."

"With that kind of philosophy, can you ever relax?"

"Sure," Gadgets replied, feeling kind of embarrassed over the questioning, the concern, shown by Babette. "Sort of."

She laughed heartily. "Tell me, Gadgets, how does a person 'sort of' relax?"

"I guess I just make sure I'm in a secure place, then I can take it easy."

She came over to him and took the gym bag off his shoulder. She set it within easy reach then moved away from him. Babette went and closed all the drapes, both in the living room and the bedroom.

"All is safe, secure. Now you can relax," she said when she returned.

"I don't know if I can relax," he said jokingly. "Somehow I get the feeling I'm under attack."

"You don't mind being under attack?" she asked, her voice a soft purr.

"No," he replied. "It's my job."

"You're tense," she said. "Your body's tight as a drum. Why don't you take off that jacket? You look hot."

And with that she started to help him out of his clothing. She took off his gaudy sport shirt, then helped him unfasten the shoulder rig. She pulled the Beretta from the rig and carefully placed the modified 93-R within easy reach of the shower stall.

"A nice hot shower will work wonders for your tension," she said as she continued undressing him. When she was finished with the Able Team warrior, she started on herself, slowly stripping the clothing from her body.

Gadgets watched, somewhat in awe. Her body, revealed to him slowly, piece of clothing by piece of clothing, was awesome. She carried no excess, only the form that had carried her to the top of the gymnastics world.

In the steaming hot shower, they lathered each other, letting their fears and tension run down the drain. Babette's touch was firm, almost harsh, her fingers digging into tense knotted muscles, loosening them, relaxing them. Gadgets performed the same intimate service for her. As the tension drained out of their bodies, as the killing and past events were forgotten, a new, wild feeling crept into their bodies.

After climbing out of the shower, Gadgets wrapped a towel around Babette. Hugging her affectionately, he helped her dry off. Drying himself, he looked again at her magnificent form. It had been ages since he had felt so warmly about a woman. His business was a cold business; to gain warmth was often to commit yourself. He could not commit himself. He had to tell Babette.

With an impatient, urgent movement, Babette touched her finger to his lips.

"Shhh," she said. "No words."

She led him to the bedroom.

13

A loud beeping broke the stale silence. Gadgets Schwarz, lying in the warm comfort of Babette Pavlovski's bed, refused to answer the summons.

"It's Pol," he said groggily.

"Well, answer it," said Babette, who had just opened her eyes, yet already looked bright, cheery.

"Can't," Gadgets complained. "Can't move. Complacency's set in."

Babette giggled, gave Gadgets a playful shove and answered the summons.

"In ten minutes," she said. "No, Pol, not alone. Both of us. Please. It's my fight. Okay."

She signed off then rolled back toward the still-dozing Gadgets. "It's time. I told him we'd be there in ten minutes."

"*We'd* be there?"

"I'm coming too, Gadgets. It's me they tried to kill. It was one of my athletes they did kill. It's my fight."

Gadgets knew better than to argue with the woman; he was smart enough not to get into fights he knew he would never win. With all the effort in the world, he dragged his butt out of bed. Babette beat him to the floorboards. She also beat him in getting dressed.

She wore tan slacks, a brown shirt and a brown patterned scarf over her hair. Gadgets hopped into the clothes he had on earlier, including the life-saving flak jacket.

"Pol says we're going to the desert," she said as they headed for the door.

"UCLA," he told the guard as they moved toward the elevator. "There'll be a chopper waiting."

When they hit the street, Gadgets looked up at the starry sky. "God," he mumbled, "what time is it?"

"Sixteen minutes after midnight," one of the Feds answered.

Ten minutes later they arrived at the helicopter. Blancanales stood waiting for them, an Ingram and a bandolier of clips for Babette in hand.

The Sikorsky H-76 was already turning over. The trio crouched as they ran under the forty-four-foot rotors. Pol climbed in a front door to the copilot seat. Gadgets and Babette went through a door farther back to the passenger compartment. The copter was lifting off before Gadgets had the door secured.

Babette took a seat. Gadgets went to the weapons boxes. He pulled off the gaudy sport shirt, electing—like his teammates—to wear a more neutrally colored flak jacket for nighttime desert fighting. He packed both hot and cold thermal packs and crisscrossed two bandoliers over his shoulders, filling the pouches with spare clips and grenades. Then he began the task of setting aside the M-16/M-79 over-and-under hybrid for Lyons. By the time he had added belts of grenades for the launcher and plenty of 5.56mm ammo for the assault rifle part, there was a mound of equipment and a web that weighed close to sixty pounds.

"What's all that for?" Babette shouted over the whine of the two Allison turboshaft engines.

"For Lyons," he replied. "He needs a lot of weight to keep his feet on the ground."

"What are you taking?" Babette asked.

"Ingram, Beretta," he answered. "Same as Pol."

They were already away from the city, surging forward at 150 knots. In an hour and twenty minutes they settled in a swirl of sand beside an identical chopper.

Lyons was in the door as soon as Blancanales opened it.

"Radio off," Lyons commanded the pilot, "unless you're wearing headphones. I don't know if the bastards are doing a radio monitor, but sound carries like crazy in the desert. Observe radio silence and noise discipline."

Lyons then looked in the back.

"What's she doing here?"

Babette came forward carrying Lyons's gear.

"I belong here," she answered, handing the Able Team warrior his tools. "They tried to kill me. They killed Tracy. Now they've got Kelly. If they had Pol or Gadgets, would you let yourself be cut out of the action?"

"I know you did a helluva job in that parking complex," Lyons said, "but our job is to keep you alive, not put you into a fire zone."

"Would you let yourself be cut out of the action?" she asked again.

"No," Lyons snapped.

"Listen," Babette said, a firmness in her voice. "I don't expect to lead the charge over the hill, but I can't be left behind either. I've got a big stake in this."

"Okay," he growled. "But your head ain't gonna be on my head. You've been warned."

Babette smiled. Gadgets and Pol shot her the thumbs-up sign.

Lyons finished arming himself to the teeth.

"STOVEPIPE WELLS, NEXT STOP," Sam Jackson announced to the others in the limousine.

"Afraid not," Boering said. He pulled the long car off the road and, for the first time, turned on the car's CB radio.

"This is Swimmer on the beach," he said. "This is Swimmer on the beach." His voice took on a clipped quality. He called about once a minute. After the third call he was greeted by a reply.

"Swimmer, this is Lifeguard," came a voice with a Georgian drawl. "Swimmer, this is Lifeguard. What's the trouble?"

"I've got five survivors. Send the lifeboats."

"This was not part of the plan," the man at the other end crackled. Anger gripped the voice.

"Just send the lifeboats. Argue later."

"Ten four," came the acknowledgment.

Lightning Sam Jackson looked at his watch. It was just past 11:30 P.M. At 11:43 he heard the roar

of dune buggies over the desert. Suddenly he saw
them sweeping over the nearest dune. Three had extra motors and propellers on the back. They looked
like something out of a science-fiction movie.

The athletes rumbled.

"What the hell's going on?" Zak Wilson asked.
"Where you taking us?"

But their fears were quickly quelled by the
smooth-talking Boering, who assured them that he
was just taking another necessary step to get them
out of the country.

On the trip to the dunes, the three props brought
up the rear, the prop wash obliterating all signs of a
trail. The buggies arrived at a camp in the dunes.
Camouflage netting covered sand buggies and nearly buried tents. Jackson pulled something from his
pocket, fiddled with it, then tossed it into the sand.

As they climbed from the buggies they were met
by a tough-looking blond man. The man looked at
Boering and then at the athletes.

"They're not in handcuffs," he stated.

"Put them somewhere for now," Boering said.
"We can't talk here."

The leader whistled and four older men materialized, pointing guns at the athletes.

"Put them in with the other guests," the leader
ordered.

"Hey! Why the guns?" Helen demanded.
"We're here voluntarily. We're not your prisoners."

One of the guards tapped her on the head with
the barrel of his automatic.

"Shut up, nigger," he said.

"No need for that," Boering snapped. He turned to the U.S. athletes. "It's just a security precaution. Please go along with it. We'll be here just a very short time."

The athletes looked at one another, but said nothing. They were herded into a large tent that was almost buried in sand.

Boering and the blond leader went over by the vehicles where they could talk in private.

"What the hell are you trying to pull?" the man said.

"Easy, Ilitch. We have our black defectors. Everything is going well. The problem is that they insisted on leaving before the Games, not after. What could I do?"

"Don't you ever call me Ilitch," the man replied. "I've been Bill Frazer for nine years. I'll remain Bill Frazer until I return to the homeland."

"Touchy," Boering noted aloud.

"You know stage two of this operation. What good will a bunch of dead American athletes do us?"

"None," Boering said. "They must be evacuated before blood time."

"And how are you going to accomplish that miracle?"

"It won't be hard, Bill. We have a ship standing by just outside territorial waters. There's a copter aboard, of course. I ordered it to arrive here at three. Load the Americans onto it and they'll be out of your hair."

"But they now know about the Zambians."

"So? When they read in the papers about the way the Americans came in here and shot up everybody, we'll have them hating their homeland. They will be much more verbal against America. It will be better than we could hope."

"I don't like it," the leader muttered. "Do you realize that if anyone was searching for the Zambians, or following the Americans, you will have led them right here?"

"I covered my steps and took all possible precautions. No one followed us here. If they find us, it'll be too late. We will have left by the time they track us down."

"Be damn careful what you say in front of the Klansmen," the leader warned. "If they find out these athletes are Americans leaving the U.S., we'll have nothing more than dead black meat to send on to Mother Russia."

"I'll watch my tongue, but you make sure nothing like that happens. That would sink this operation."

The blond-haired mole nodded. He did not need to be reminded that a sunk operation usually ended with a bullet to the head.

"I'm going back to Los Angeles now," Boering said. "I wouldn't want anyone to miss me. Just get those Americans on that copter when it lands. It will need instructions. You have the frequency?"

Ilitch nodded.

IT WAS DARK INSIDE the tent. The American athletes could not make out the new surroundings they had been placed in. They took small, tentative steps and encountered bodies stretched out on all sides. They were barely in the tent, but could find no space to move.

"Anyone alive in here?" Sam Jackson asked, almost afraid of the answer.

"That you, Sam?" a tentative female voice answered.

"Kelly?" Sam asked.

"Yeah, it's me," she replied.

"Who's with you?" asked a rumbling voice from close to Kelly.

"A few buddies," Sam said. "No gunmen, relax. Is that you, Mustav?"

"Got that one right, little man."

"Make room for these people," Mustav ordered. "And let's sing a hymn of rejoicing for our brothers—sing it just loud enough that those outside cannot hear our conversation."

There was a great deal of shuffling and shifting. It was like a small reunion of friends, many of whom had not seen one another since the international meet at Montreal.

Kelly, Sam and Mustav put their heads close together so they could hear one another's voices over the singing.

Kelly asked if Jackson knew anything about Babette.

"She's okay," Jackson said. The boxer then got down to business.

"Some blond guy sent us out here to find you."

"What are you talking about?" a relieved Kelly asked.

"Some blond-haired guy. I don't really know who he is. He's got something to do with Olympic security and I heard some guys—two guys he hangs around with—call him Lyons. I'll tell you, he's one mean mother. I wouldn't want him against me."

"Sounds like one of the guys I met at the airport," Kelly said.

"He was definitely at the airport with you," Jackson said. "He told us about you getting on the bus after you spotted something strange coming down."

"I knew something weird was happening and I wanted to be with Mustav, but I sure didn't figure they were going to start gunning at people."

"Anyway," Sam said, "seems you forgot to throw bread crumbs out the window so this Lyons could follow you. So he got us to find you."

"How'd you do that?" Kelly asked.

"We defected—as much as an American can defect. It was Lyons's idea. We told Boering we'd leave the U.S. but only if he could get us out immediately. We put as much pressure on him as possible. He went for it. Lyons figured he wouldn't be able to get us out right away so he said the bastard would bring us here as a stopover. Now old Boering's heading back to L.A.—to a hotel room full of cops."

"What good does it do anyone to have you guys held captive here with us?" Mustav asked.

"We carried bugs. Lyons and his partners will find us now."

"You mean they didn't check you?" Kelly questioned.

"God, yeah. Boering's a suspicious man. He checked us twice, but this guy—Gadgets or something—planted a couple of bugs on the car for Boering to find. He thinks this Gadgets is dead. He expected somebody to bug the car so he had an ambush waiting. I don't know if he made it or not."

"If they had an ambush waiting for him," Mustav said, "he's probably dead."

"Don't bet on it," Jackson said. "Earlier, this Gadgets and another guy, Pol, were waiting for Babette to come back to the team. So was a motorcycle gang of thirty or forty men. Babette and the two made it to the parking building. They killed off about half the gang before Lyons and some tactical squad came in and mopped up."

"Okay, so they're good, and tough," Mustav conceded. "How are they going to find us if they scanned you twice for bugs?"

"We were each given one to carry. They had on-and-off switches, something this Gadgets guy devised. Whenever Boering reached for the bug sniffer, we turned the bugs off. I thought we'd be searched here. I tossed my bug into the sand."

By this time Jackson's eyes had adjusted to the darkness. He could see sand had been piled up in one area.

"Mind telling me about the sand castle you're building?"

"We've burrowed below the sandbags in three places," Mustav explained. "We've been going in and out of here for hours. We wait until one of the guards is distracted, then someone slips out. They'll see the digging in the morning, but we don't figure we'll last much longer than that if we don't do something.''

"Sounds positive.''

"Listen, Sam. When they brought us here, no one covered their faces. We could identify any of those guys. They know it. We know it.''

"I don't think they'll do anything until they get us out of here," Sam said. "I think they really want us to go Commie. It'll look good for their system and look like shit on ours. They paid me good money, and I don't think they did it just to kill me.''

"We're waiting for them to settle in and get bored," Mustav told the boxer. "Your arrival stirred things up. Soon as it settles we'll start slipping out again one at a time. The first time they see anybody, we charge.''

"That's suicide," Sam said.

"So is just sitting here waiting," Kelly countered.

"Why not wait for those dudes to come?'' Jackson asked.

"No," Mustav said, his voice firm, his mind made up. "The plan goes ahead.''

"Okay," Jackson said. "You really figure all those guys out there are Ku Klux Klan?''

"Seem to be," Kelly answered. "Except for a couple of the young ones. They don't fit the mold. Everybody noticed.''

"Something still stinks," Jackson said. "It just doesn't make sense. Any Klansman I've ever heard of would rather kiss a black than help a Commie.

No matter how I pile this, I get a load of shit."

"Either some of these guys are KKK or they're damn good at faking it," Kelly said. "Or, maybe most are KKK and they don't know there's any Communist involvement. Listen, if these guys are genuine KKK, they'd rather associate with us subhumans than Communists."

Mustav picked up on the idea. "We can continue to try and sneak out of here. At the same time, let's pick the most likely candidate and tell him that Sam and his group are Americans. If he goes through the roof, we'll know they're the real thing."

The threesome planned and plotted some more. Mustav then passed the word around that the singing could stop.

Sam Jackson listened as the voices died out and silence took over. The big boxer had a small plan of his own. He could hardly wait for the gunmen outside to settle down. Then he'd make his move.

ANATOLI RUSTOV DID NOT RECEIVE his briefing from the captain of the Soviet spy ship; the instructions came directly from Portisch, the Party representative on board.

"We will go directly up to that little tub and raise hell," Portisch said. "Simply fly straight east. The bulk of the ship will cut off their radar. They won't be able to hear you over the noise of our speakers. The captain will make sure that there is plenty of noise. He wishes to return to Russia some day.

"When you approach the land radar, we have two small planes set to attract the attention of all the radars—they'll look like they are going to crash. When you get to the desert region you'll get the homing signal. It will sound like two radio amateurs chattering. There's gasoline at the pickup point, but you shouldn't need it.

"Pick up the athletes and get out of there quickly. At dawn there will be an airborne attack on the camp. If you're still there, you can expect to be eliminated.

"Is all that clear?"

"Yes, sir," Rustov answered.

"Good. On the way out, be careful. If you're spotted, run for it. Once you set down on this ship they won't touch you. A chase, by the way, would make good press. Five of their top athletes are leaving their country just before the Games. And the mighty U.S.A. is reduced to chasing them to try and stop them...."

"I'll get them here," Rustov vowed.

"Excellent, comrade. With people like you serving our nation, there can be no doubt we will soon rule these soft imperialists."

14

Gadgets Schwarz would have run right into the guard if the goon hadn't fired the cigarette. But the sentry had given away his position with the flick of a match, and Gadgets, who had one ear wired into the directional finder as he homed in on the squealers, backed off. The guard was only ten feet away.

Moving away from the guard, Gadgets went back to his teammates. The three men of Able Team and Babette Pavlovski flopped into the sand and wormed their way back over the nearest dune.

"See anything besides the sentry?" Blancanales asked.

"Barbed wire and camouflage netting," Gadgets answered.

"We'll have to go in soft at first," Pol stated.

"You know what I think about going in soft," Lyons muttered. The warrior was aching for action. "I'll go in," he volunteered.

"Take Babette with you," Politician directed. "She's the one all the athletes will recognize. Gadgets can monitor the radio and I'll take the combo, in case we hit heavy action."

All agreed. Lyons shucked most of his heavy gear

and began to crawl over the dune. Gadgets put a hand on Babette's arm before she could follow.

"Take a knife," he said.

She shook her head and whispered. "Where I was brought up, young girls are all taught to wear this." She guided his hand to her forearm. Strapped in a leather sheath was an old-fashioned ice pick. "It's the only way to say no to a Russian soldier."

She gave him a quick peck on the cheek and was gone.

Lyons crawled rapidly toward the glow of the cigarette. He paused under an accordion roll of barbed wire, trusting its lines to break his outline against the sand. A light tap on his boot told him where Babette was.

Lyons and Babette began a slow circling of the enclosure. Iron posts, driven deep into the sand, supported both the overhead netting and the rolls of razor-sharp wire. The rolls had been laid into a trench and the sand had been allowed to drift back in to cover the bottom foot of the rolls. It was not much of an anchor, but enough to slow someone making a run for it from inside.

The dune buggies, parked closely together, did not provide a sheltered spot for entry. They were not up to the wire, and a sentry patrolled the area between the buggies and the wire. The gate had a guard seated on each end. It was festooned with wire, but made to swing clear of the sand. Like the rest of the perimeter it was designed only to slow people down if they tried to escape—not to protect against outer attack. The gate was about four feet high, eight feet wide.

Lyons crawled straight back from the gate until he was behind a dune. Babette soon slid behind him.

"I don't see any damn way in there that is quiet," he whispered.

SAM JACKSON CRAWLED PARTWAY through the door of the tent. As soon as he saw the guard facing him, he knew what Kelly had meant by the young men who did not fit the KKK mold. This sentry was alert, hard, a lot like the man who had met them when they entered the camp.

"You want something, boy?" the guard asked, his voice thick with contempt.

"Gotta piss, man," Jackson replied in a similar tone.

"Baker," the guard called. Another man materialized from the darkness. He was about forty-five, supporting a beer-and-pizza potbelly, and displaying none of the military alertness shown by the younger man.

"This nigger's gotta piss. Hold his hand."

Baker gestured for Jackson to move toward the farthest end of the compound. The boxer walked ahead of the guard, then slowed down. From the distance behind them, a gruff voice called, "And, Baker, make sure that's all you hold." The comment was followed by a vicious laugh.

"Asshole," Baker muttered under his breath.

When Jackson and Baker were far enough away

from the other sentry, Jackson made his pitch. "Why you guys want to do this to American athletes just before the Games? You don't give a shit for the flag?"

"Don't bullshit me, Zambian."

"Zambian? I was with the last group. American, man. And we're being blackmailed into leaving so Russia can win the Games, and so Russia can spit on America."

"Boy," Baker said. "If you gotta piss, go over to that pit. If you wanna talk, talk to your nigger friends."

"Thought a man like you'd be a boxing fan."

"I like the fights," Baker answered. "What about it?"

"Thought you'd recognize the U.S. amateur champion."

"Sam Jackson? Lightning Sam Jackson?"

"You're looking at him."

The guard looked confused. He stared at Jackson, trying to get a good look at his face in the poor light. Recognition flickered in his eyes, but he did not admit it.

"You, ahh, are kinda big. And you do.... Shit. Lotta people look like other people."

"Believe what you want then, man," Jackson said as he finished relieving himself. "I just know who I am and I sure as hell don't want to go to Russia. But if you want to send me...."

"Shut up," the guard said as he started to move back toward the tent. Jackson knew he had planted the seed.

When he pulled beside the young guard at the door of the tent, Jackson whirled. "Hey," he said in a loud voice, "I saw you and that Communist swim coach talking a couple weeks back. You work for the Commies."

The guard's M-16 swung at Sam's head. The boxer ducked. "He's trying to kill me," he said.

While checking the swing of the assault rifle, the guard shot his right foot in a lashing karate kick at Jackson's crotch. The fighter barely had time to turn and take the kick on the hip. The blow was strong enough to send him staggering. This gave the guard time to sweep the rifle back to target on Jackson.

The powerful black boxer saw the M-16 barrel coming. He knew he had to make a larger scene if anyone was going to escape under the tent. He also knew he was toying with his life.

"Help!" he screamed. At the same moment he took a long dive, out of the line of the swinging barrel. He tucked and rolled at the end of his dive, stopping against a pair of boots. The owner of those boots held a knife to his throat. It was Bill Frazer, the guncock who had met Boering when the American athletes were brought to the camp.

Sam Jackson lay still. "I'll go with you. I'll leave America," he said. "Just don't kill me. Don't use the knife."

The boxer believed his performance was strong enough to make the KKK men realize he was American, not Zambian. He also believed he had made a fatal mistake. He saw the knifeholder's jaw snap shut. He knew the goon would now kill him for spilling the truth. Jackson wrenched his body to one side as the knife plunged into the sand where his throat had been just a second before.

THE INSTANT JACKSON HAD SAID: "Hey, I saw you..." both Babette and Lyons had stuck their heads over the top of the dune. Babette thrust her Ingram at Lyons and took off running down the side of the dune by the gate. Lyons watched the woman, who seemed to have suicidal tendencies. He slid the silenced 93-R from leather and took a steady two-handed grip, resting his arms on the top of the dune. Then he waited, his face a grim mask of concentration.

The guard at the hinge end of the gate was slim, the one at the latch end was grossly overweight. The fat slob advanced a few steps when he heard the sound of footsteps. In an easy dive, Babette slammed into the thin guard. Before he could react, an ice pick was sliding between his ribs; it stopped upon impact with the heart. A small but firm hand remained over the guard's mouth until the violent thrashing slowly died.

When Sam Jackson yelled for help, the Beretta coughed. The pudgy guard dropped onto his face. Warm blood filtered into the fine sand. The slob died with grit covering his eyes, nose and mouth. He let out no sound.

Babette dragged the thin guard over to the dune buggies and stuffed him under the nearest vehicle. By the time she was finished, Lyons had let himself into the compound and was using the rope that had held the gate to tie the other guard to an iron post near the gate. He tied the man in an on-duty standing position. Lyons turned to hand Babette her gun, but she had remained by the buggies. Her head was cocked as she listened intently. The Able Team warrior went over to her.

"Someone saw me hiding the body," she whispered. "Whoever it is is hiding around the cars."

Lyons nodded and began to skirt the buggies, hoping to cut the person off from getting back to the rest of the camp. As he crouch-walked around the vehicles he became aware that someone was stalking him. He quickly checked; he could still make out Babette holding her position. Someone else was on his ass.

SAM JACKSON TRIED TO CONTINUE his roll and get back on his feet. Another pair of boots halted his movement. He looked up into the scowling face of Baker, the guard whom he had tried to recruit.

Baker looked at the knife man. "Easy, Bill, we're supposed to keep them alive."

He bent down and grabbed the boxer by the collar. With Jackson's help, he got the big man back on his feet. Baker put his face next to Jackson's, trying to make out the features.

"Isn't this one of the special ones who's supposed to be taken out by copter?" Baker asked.

"How'd you know that?" Frazer snapped. He still held the bowie knife and he still looked ready to use it.

"He told me," Baker answered in an innocent voice. Now he was sure the boxer hadn't been lying.

"Yeah," Frazer said, "the ones who just came are to be moved somewhere else. But that don't mean he ain't expendable."

With a sudden, quick movement, Baker had Jackson's arm bent behind his back and jammed up his spine. "You come quiet," Baker warned. "I'm a former cop and I haven't forgotten how to bust a thick skull."

Jackson stumbled ahead of the man, feeling more helpless than before. Unless this Baker dude was feigning loyalty, he figured sooner or later someone was going to slit his throat. When they reached the door of the tent, the guard gave Jackson a shove that sent him sprawling on his face. Baker left and the boxer sat up to massage the tender muscles in his shoulder.

"You're lacking terribly in the brains department," said a rumbling voice from the far side of the tent. "But I know four men would thank you for what you did."

"Four men got out," Jackson said. "Mustav, man, that news makes the risk worthwhile."

The boxer crawled over to one of the water containers and toasted his success with a drink of warm, metallic-tasting water. As he was putting the cap back on the container, he heard voices outside. Someone whispered his name. He went to the door.

A guard stood at the flap. Jackson suspected it was the ex-cop, but he couldn't be sure. The figure gestured for him to come out. Jackson started toward the man. The second he cleared the tent, four pair of hands reached out of the darkness and seized him. Before he could react, a patch of adhesive tape had been slapped over his mouth and his hands had been forced behind him and cuffed. He was swept off his feet and quickly carted away.

A voice whispered in his ear.

"Struggle, nigger. Or make a sound. Or just breathe wrong. I'll take great pleasure in clubbing you to death."

Out of the corner of his eye, Sam Jackson spotted the solid-looking butt of a gun.

THE FAINT SOUND OF SAND being finely shifted by a foot told Carl Lyons to kiss the earth. He dropped flat on his face as a tire iron sliced air above his head. Lyons rolled over, his drawn Beretta questing a target.

The target was clearly outlined against the bright stars. Lyons held his fire. His attacker was a black man with a wild afro.

"Drop it," Lyons ordered. He tried to put the man's mind at ease. "I'm a friend. I'm with Babette Pavlovski."

The black man clutched the tire iron as if it was his last hope for freedom. But the athlete knew that if he used the weapon, the man with the gun would rearrange his face.

The athlete eased back, dropped the tire iron. Lyons motioned for him to retreat to where Babette was waiting. Babette—showing the love that runs deep in the athletic community—hugged the man.

The two exchanged whispers. Then Babette let the man go and he disappeared into the heap of dune buggies. The gymnastics coach crept back to the gate.

Babette returned to Lyons, carrying the guns that belonged to the dead guards. Two black athletes materialized from the night and took the guns. Another conversation followed and the two blacks casually walked up to the gate. They untied the body of the dead guard, shoved it between two buggies and took the place of the guards. Lyons signaled for Babette to follow him and they began moving farther into the camp.

Slowly they worked their way around the parked dune buggies and past a small tent and some sort of plank shack almost buried completely in the sand. They stopped beside the largest tent in the camp. A sentry was sitting at table. The approach to him was open sand. Lyons picked himself up and began walking toward him. If Babette Pavlovski could try suicide tactics, so could Carl Lyons.

"Who's that?" the guard challenged, bringing his weapon up.

"Shut the fuck up," Lyons whispered as he walked confidently toward the guard. "I brought you some refreshment."

Lyons had one arm behind his back as though he were hiding a bottle. With a quick, powerful uppercut, he brought the hand up. By the time his fist hit the guard square in the mouth, he had all his force planted in his rising arm. When his fist connected he could hear the shatter of bones. He could feel the guard's face collapsing. He could not remember ever having hit a man so hard, so deadly. The sentry dropped in a bloodied heap on the sand. Lyons rubbed his aching knuckles.

Babette gave him a hand placing the body underneath the roll of barbed wire. The duo then went to the side of the tent. Babette, having talked with the athletes, knew where the tunnel was. She went first and was followed by Lyons. Inside the tent he was met by blackness. Absolute blackness.

Babette's voice came from behind him.

"Kelly."

"Who's that?" a female voice answered.

"Kelly," Babette said, putting a little more volume in her voice. "You're breaking training."

Kelly let out a giggle before instructing Lyons and Babette to join her and Mustav, who were sitting about ten feet away. Introductions and a warm reunion followed.

"The guard on the side of the tent where we came in had an accident," Lyons said to Mustav. "Get one of your men out there to take his place. We've already got two of your guys on the gate."

Mustav balked. "Lyons," he said, "our men will not stand up to scrutiny."

"I don't want them to. If they're caught we're at war. Hopefully by them standing there we can buy a little time."

Mustav issued orders.

"How big a force do you have out there?" he then asked Lyons.

Lyons refused to answer. He knew that if he

talked about the small numbers the athletes would be dispirited. They had no way of knowing the power the small force was capable of.

He veered onto another topic.

"Where's Jackson?"

"We're worried about him," Kelly answered. "Someone called for him and when he went to the door he was taken away. We figure the KKK goons can't be knowingly involved with Russia. Sam was trying to get them to help us."

"Oh, God," Babette moaned.

Although the athletes' hunch agreed with his own, Lyons did not think too much of Jackson's chances. He said nothing of his doubts.

"We'd better act fast," Lyons told the others. "But try not to get into some damn shooting war as long as we can take over slowly with guerrilla tactics."

Before the Able Team fighter could continue, Zak Wilson let out a low whistle from the front of the tent. A rustling filled the tent as someone moved. Lyons was pushed, driven backward. He struggled to bring the Beretta up on the attackers but Babette was pushed into him. A pair of flashlights shone into the entry of the tent.

Lyons and Pavlovski, not wanting to be found in the tent, kept low, away from the action.

"Someone called Mustav. Someone called Kelly," a southern voice drawled. "Sam Jackson wants you."

The flashlights began to play over the bodies on the crowded sand floor. Athletes immediately scrambled to their feet, trying to keep the light from reaching the evidence of their digging, trying to distract the flashlight carriers. The huge Zambian and Kelly quickly stepped forward.

"Mustav and Kelly," the weight lifter said to the white man.

"Jackson said you'd be the biggest man here. Move ahead of us."

The two captors took a step to each side to let the two athletes past.

"One question," Mustav rumbled. "What in hell's going on?"

"Jackson says the last group delivered here are Americans being blackmailed to leave America. We say he's a lying shit. We don't believe him. He says you can convince us. We'll give you one chance, nigger."

When they had left, Lyons whispered to Babette. "Make your way back to Pol and Gadgets. The three of you then come in by the gate. We're going to have to risk commando tactics."

Babette left the tent. Lyons instructed the others.

"Wait here until weapons start being delivered. Keep three armed fighters inside to guard the rest. After that, every time someone is armed, he should get out to join the fight. Use our people on guard duty to connect with our people outside. And listen, I know most of you have never fired a gun. Christ, most of you've never held a gun. One thing you've gotta remember—a gun can talk without being fired. At least if you're holding a gun you've got a hope."

Lyons ducked out of the tent. He raised his head slowly on the outside. It would be dawn soon and the action had to go down before then. Any moment they might change the guard, or inspect it.

Moving low but fast, Lyons caught sight of the four Klansman hauling Kelly and Mustav away. When they had disappeared into another buried tent, he noted their position, then doubled back. He was close to the captives' tent when he saw something move. He watched for a second before realizing it was a guard, following Babette.

Babette moved forward, the guard followed and Lyons followed the guard, trying to gain some precious ground before the bastard had a chance to ambush the woman. Suddenly, out of the corner of his eye, Lyons saw another sentry zeroing in on Babette. Lyons had to slow down to allow the man to close the gap between himself and Babette. The Able Team warrior moved in behind him.

Lyons pulled a garrote from one of the pockets in his flak jacket. As the figure moved unsuspectingly along, Lyons caught him from behind. He crossed his wrists as he wrapped the garrote around the man's neck. The wire loop began its brutal, cutting justice. The ambusher, with his final burst of energy, wildly swung his arm back. Lyons moved to one side but not before a knife sliced through his thigh.

A breath escaped from a hole Lyons had produced in the man's throat. He squeezed until the cold clutch of the garrote tore the life from the goon.

Lyons let the man drop. In that instant he felt the

barrel of a cocked revolver touching his temple. It was one of the athletes. Out of the corner of his eye he could see that Babette was safe. An athlete posing as a guard was lifting the barbed wire with his assault rifle so that the gymnastics coach could crawl under. A felled gunman was by the foot of the athlete.

"Okay," the athlete whispered when he got close enough to identify Lyons. He let his gun arm drop. Lyons liked his style.

"Take care of him," Lyons ordered.

The athlete carefully stripped the body of weapons and ammunition. While the man delivered the weapons to the tent, Lyons dropped his pants to assess damage. The cut was about six inches long but not deep enough to have done any permanent muscle damage. He pulled his pants back up and blocked out the pain. He'd lived with deeper wounds; he'd fought with deeper wounds.

The athlete came back and hid the body. Lyons tested his leg, tentatively at first, then with all his power. The leg held up. He headed for the tent where Jackson, Mustav and Kelly were being questioned.

En route he thought about Able Team's biggest problem. Taking the camp normally would have been easy. Defensively, the place was a joke. Christ, Lyons thought, it was as if the place had been designed to be taken. The problem was how to do it without getting the athletes killed.

Lyons was within twenty feet of the tent when a four-man squad moved silently in front of him. He crouched low as the men moved past him toward the tent. The Able Team member faded back a few steps.

The four men surrounded the tent. The man who was leading the squad stood in front of the tent flaps. Lyons figured out what was coming down. He waited.

"Who's in there?" the head man called.

The muttering inside the tent died.

"Is that you out there, Bill?" a voice called back. "Come on in. Me and Terry just questioning some niggers."

"It is me, Baker. But I ain't coming in, you're coming out. All of you with your hands above your heads."

"Hey, Bill. Jesus. What's got the burr in your saddle?" Baker called out. "We're not doing anything to them. Look out for yourself."

"If you're not out in five seconds, we'll fire through the tent. One . . . two . . . three . . . ."

Lyons took three steps forward, the silenced Beretta in his fist. He folded down the second handgrip and hooked his thumb through the front of the trigger guard. With a two-handed grip—crouching for maximum steadiness—he fired three shots.

Three of the guncocks went down. The fourth, known as Bill Frazer, had homed in on the barely audible sound. His Colt New Service M1917 swung to bear on the source.

Lyons swung the 93-R, targeting on his fourth hit. The last casing had stovepiped. In the darkness he could not see the frontsight for the shell stuck between the breech and the receiver. He squeezed the trigger, letting instinct aim, then flung himself to one side.

The Colt barked three times, its death messengers driving into sand, almost catching up with the diving Lyons. The Beretta had probably picked up sand, Lyons thought as his body crashed to the dirt. He bounced slightly, hoping he could stay clear of the incoming .45s until he could clear the jam.

The three unmuffled shots had roused the entire camp.

Lyons figured he had only seconds before the camp was transformed into a shooting gallery, using athletes as targets.

Lyons figured his own chances for survival were slim.

15

Colonel Frank Follet figured he had the world exactly where he wanted it. He would achieve two victories at once. He bent again to examine the blips on the radar screen. He would prove his genius for command and take care of that interfering goon from Washington all in one shot—and he'd do so now.

The radio operator was speaking. "We have you on the screen, interceptor two. Stand by for orders."

Follet took the microphone from the operator and directed the interceptor pilot. "Keep the helicopter in sight. Let it get over land and away from the city, then force it down. Do you read that. Force it down."

"I read," the pilot answered.

Follet turned to the other radio operator. "Take an immediate message to all area commanders."

"Yes, sir."

"An enemy aircraft has breached U.S. airspace. Further report on the aircraft will follow."

"Is that it, sir?"

"That's it. Sign it Acting Commander F. Follet. And get it out now."

"Yes, sir."

Follet turned his attention to the first radio tech. "Get those two Sikorskys back here. I don't care who this Lyons has backing him. I've got an enemy craft breaching U.S. airspace. I'm in command."

The operator tried to reach the helicopters. Follet stood behind him, smiling, dreaming dreams of being made a general.

"I can't seem to raise them, sir. They're not responding."

As the radio man watched the red creep into Follet's neck and face, he was glad of the hours he had spent practicing darts. He was the second best dart thrower on the base and at this moment he felt it was the only thing that stood between himself and a dishonorable discharge. Most of all, he was glad he had had the sense that had told him to throw his last match with Colonel Follet.

"Keep trying and let me know the moment you've ordered them back."

"Yes, sir."

Follet stormed out of communications.

"Whew," exclaimed one operator. "Wonder what that Lyons did?"

"Whatever he did in the past," the dart chucker replied, "it ain't nothing compared to spoiling old Follet's victory. Whoever this Lyons is, I hope he's got the sense to disappear."

BILL FRAZER NEVER HAD A CHANCE to fire a fourth shot at the sprawling Lyons. Klansman Baker and Sam Jackson erupted from the tent like two human cannonballs. Baker hit the guy's ankles while Jackson hit him high and hard. As the man was going down, Jackson punched him in the face.

Lyons got up, worked the slide on the Beretta. The stovepiped shell flew clear, but he would not be confident of the weapon until he could strip and relube it.

Kelly, Mustav and another Klansman came scrambling out of the tent. Baker and Jackson got up off the ground. Baker went and looked at one of the silenced bodies. He waved his hand to the athletes and Lyons.

"Fade," he spat, "out of sight before there's a bloodbath."

KKK forces were already streaming toward the place where the shots had sounded. The foursome dropped and crawled away as quickly as possible. They moved until they were away from the tent, then turned to watch what was happening.

"Quiet down," Baker hollered over the babble of questions being thrown at him. "I'm not sure what the hell happened. Me and Terry were in the tent when Bill Frazer came and shouted for us to come out. He said he had the tent surrounded and would shoot if we didn't . . . ."

"I heard that part," a voice chimed in.

"I told Bill to come in and that nothing was wrong," Baker continued. "But he wouldn't. Me and Terry were coming out when somebody shot these poor bastards. Bill was shooting away like a madman so we tackled him and knocked him out."

One of the guards was inspecting the hit gunmen.

"Jonesy. He's dead," he said. The other two men were identified and confirmed dead. Baker and Terry both offered their guns for inspection. It was agreed—the only gun that had been fired was Bill Frazer's.

A voice lifted above the others. "I don't buy none of this shit. It's all fishy as hell."

The man on the ground moaned. "He's coming around," Baker said. "Why don't you ask him?"

Everyone gathered around the fallen man. Jackson and Kelly took the opportunity to crawl back to the tent and grab the guns off the dead men.

"What happened, Bill?" someone asked.

The reply was mumbled and incomprehensible. The fallen man shook his head, tried to clear the cobwebs.

Suddenly he looked up. "Where's the nigger who hit me?"

"What nigger?" Terry asked. The question was fired too quickly.

"I heard talking in the tent. Baker and Terry were inside. Claimed they were questioning niggers. I told them to come out with their hands up."

He paused to take a few deep breaths. The men began to mutter among themselves. Suspicion hung onto their voices.

While the KGB hardman, posing as a Klansman, continued to speak, Jackson and Kelly crawled back to Lyons and Mustav. They carried the guns taken from the dead men. Once back they found positions five feet to either side of Lyons. The three kept their weapons trained on the gathering.

Lyons pulled back to Mustav. "Get everyone out of that tent. Fast," he whispered. Mustav nodded.

A voice cut the night air.

"Somebody's got Jonesy's Colt!"

The man who had not been buying Baker's story from the beginning grabbed the former lawman's shirt. He put a handgun to Baker's chin.

"You're lying," the hardman spat. "You've got a second to come up with the truth, assho—"

His words were chewed by the bullet fired by Carl Lyons. The Able Team sharpshooter had hoped like hell that his gun would be able to give him an accurate shot. He had hoped like hell and then he had acted. He'd had to try, it was their only hope. The Beretta's bullet pounded the man's face to a bloody pulp. He dropped in an instant. Baker had bought a little bit of life.

Lyons lifted, eyes searching for the KGB mole, searching for Bill Frazer. He was the chief danger. The scene was highly explosive, and Frazer was the fuse.

A bullet from a perimeter guard tugged at his earlobe.

He cursed the bastard, then killed him with a burst to the chest.

"Machine-gun the niggers before they overrun us." Frazer's voice boomed over the chaos. "Machine-gun the niggers."

Lyons sprinted to intercept the KGB killer. His cut thigh fired shots of pain through his entire lower body. He ignored the pain and pressed on. His battle senses working overtime, he heard, between violent tugs of breath, a slow-flying twin-prop plane going overhead.

There was sporadic firing from the perimeter. Lyons was close enough to see muzzle flashes coming from the gate and the west side of the prisoners' tent. Athletes, knowing it was a matter of kill or be killed, were picking off anyone who was prepared to carry out Frazer's orders.

Just ahead of him, Lyons saw the KGB goon raise his automatic to bear on the tent. Lyons fired on the run. The shot took the mole from behind, entering at the base of the skull and driving, plowing its way through the brain. Bill Frazer, once a KGB mole, dropped to the ground, now dead. His blood and brains mixed in a gory concoction on the battleground.

Lyons stopped and reversed his ground. He headed back toward the tent where Jackson, Mustav and Kelly had been held. Behind the tent, Baker was shouting to make himself heard over the yapping and confusion.

"There's some sort of crack response team inside our camp right now. They're after the hostages and the goddamn Commies."

"As long as we've got the hostages, we're okay," another Klan member yelled.

"Bullshit," Baker said. "As long as we've got the hostages we're at war."

"I say we kill the Commies that conned us," another said.

"Most are dead," Baker said, nodding at the dead men on the ground.

Lyons heard the chopping-air sound of a copter landing. He figured it was about a half-mile off.

"Listen," Baker reasoned, "I've been told if we release the hostages, we'll be disarmed and sent back to L.A. with the athletes. They want the KGB ringleaders, not us. We're small potatoes."

A bullet snapped at Lyons, barely missing. He turned to shoot, but automatic fire from outside the perimeter cut the gunner to shreds.

The rest of Able Team had arrrived.

The KKK members continued arguing. The shooting had nearly stopped, save for the odd person acting on a nervous impulse. Lyons stood covering the scene with a Beretta. Anyone made a wrong move, he would personally make them pay.

The argument seemed to be going nowhere. Most believed they had been conned by KGB moles, but a course of action could not be decided upon. They knew a small but powerful team was in the camp, and they knew many athletes had acquired guns and were ready to fight. The death toll would be high, but. . . could anybody be trusted to set them free? If not, they would fight.

"Jesus," a voice said. Lyons looked to his left. Lightning Sam Jackson was striking. Slowly he moved toward the mob of Klansmen. He tossed his captured handgun to Lyons and walked on with his hands in the air. "People gonna die if you don't quit pissin' around," he said to the Klansmen. Lyons couldn't believe his eyes. In all his years of wars, never. . . . The big boxer strode right into the pack and started playing arbitrator. With his quick tongue he was negotiating for his side, their side, Able Team's side—for peace.

Lyons knelt and watched Jackson. He had the boxer's Browning Hi-Power. He placed it between his knees, ready to grab it in an instant. Then, he field stripped the Beretta, his fingers carefully checking each part. He removed grains of sand with his fingernails as he put the parts back together. It wasn't the sort of strip down the gun really needed, but it would have to do.

Lyons kept the reassembled Beretta in his fist, but tucked away the silencer. The time for delicacy had long passed. Dawn was slowly creeping onto the horizon.

"Lyons," a woman whispered.

Babette jogged over to him, keeping low. She was laden with most of his gear. Lyons stood and quickly donned his web belt and two bandoliers. The M-16/M-79 felt reassuring in his hands. The Able Team member's eyes never left the group that now surrounded Sam Jackson. Whatever it was the boxer was selling, the Klansmen seemed to be buying. Lyons listened while trying to locate Pol and Gadgets outside the perimeter.

Suddenly an automatic rifle opened up from just outside the compound, raking the group around Jackson. Lyons swung toward the muzzle flash. Another gun spoke. In the split second that followed, Lyons could hear the bullets impact on a human body. He searched for the source. The second gun carried the slower, more deliberate voice of a Stony Man modified automatic. An unknown had fired into the compound and an Able Team member had instantly answered.

Standing next to the compound, Blancanales shouted. "Enemy forces closing in. Everyone out this way. It's a trap."

The Ingram spoke again. From the same spot, Gadgets let out another word. "Hurry!"

The encampment was thrown into a state of confusion.

Lyons sprinted toward the group sprawled in the sand around the mouth of the tent. Two KKK members were dead, both having taken bullets to the chest.

"Prop up that wire and get out that way," he yelled, pointing in the direction where he had heard Schwarz and Blancanales calling from.

Lyons handed the Browning back to Jackson. Jackson summoned Mustav. "Get your buddies moving this way," he instructed. "Let's go."

Another automatic weapon began emptying into the compound. Answering fire blasted from several places, but it was the authoritative boom of a twelve-gauge that silenced the killer automatic.

"It's your goddamn men firing at us," an angry Klansman shouted as he attacked Lyons. The Able Team member feinted a move to the right then quickly countered with a kick at the man's testicles. He connected and the man went down in a heap of agony.

"Listen, asshole," Lyons said, grabbing the fallen goon by the shirt. "If my men were firing this way—with me standing here—I'd personally cut their hands off." Lyons pushed the man's head back to the pillow of sand.

The display had been both impressive and convincing. Lyons's quick action and the immediate response from the athletes had given the Klansmen a course to follow. Their only other option was to die in a state of confusion. Both blacks and whites threw themselves on their stomachs and crawled under the wires. Pol stood at the opening, giving instructions to each person who crawled through. Gadgets led the column toward the helicopters.

Babette moved up beside Lyons.

"Search this area quickly, then get out," Lyons said. "I'd never want to have to defend this place. I swear it was set up not to be defended."

Lyons glanced up to the horizon. Dawn was coloring the landscape. The first light of morning silhouetted the dunes to the east.

"We'll be sitting ducks in five, ten minutes. Get four people to help you. Make that search as fast as possible."

An enemy voice shouted in alarm. "They're escaping...."

It was cut off by a single shot.

Lyons ran to the area where everyone was escaping. Baker stood over the body of another dead Klansman. "They got another," he said. "Everyone else's accounted for. Doubt we'll ever make it out though."

"Paratroopers haven't had a chance to get organized," Lyons said. "We'll...."

A sudden burst of fire dug sand beside them. One

member of the enemy had come close enough to kill. Lyons pointed the combo weapon at the muzzle flash and sent a stream of tumblers in a four-leaf-clover pattern. The next sound from the desert was that of death. The enemy's vocal cords struggled with the fact that half his chest had been blown away.

Lyons heard a mild groan even closer to home. He looked down at the ex-cop, the KKK man who led the revolt against the KGB moles. Baker had stopped a bullet. He was dying slowly. Lyons moved over to the Klansman. Blood was trickling out the side of his mouth, down his chin. He gazed up at Lyons, a glazed look in his eyes.

"Forgive..." he said, and then death snatched the sentence from his mouth.

Dawn had opened up a small patch of sky, but the dunes surrounding the encampment and the camouflage netting held the dark. Lyons scoured the perimeter, looking for those paratroopers who had managed to make it that far, that fast.

Gadgets Schwarz crawled over the last sand dune between the line of retreat and the helicopters. There was enough light to outline each person scrambling after him over the sand. They would be ideal targets for anyone coming across their flank.

Years of being on constant alert had conditioned the warrior in Gadgets. He knew time had sided with the unknown enemy, but he did not run and hail the copters. Instead, he approached cautiously.

The two Sikorsky H-76s were sitting side by side. Gadgets signaled for those behind him to wait. He skirted the choppers; in the small space between them he saw the two pilots being interrogated at gunpoint by four rough-looking gunmen.

Gadgets hurried back to the line of Klansmen and athletes. He whispered terse instructions. Armed men disappeared right and left, circling the choppers. Gadgets approached the enemy from the side, keeping the nearest Sikorsky between himself and the enemy. Ten feet from the large helicopter he went to his stomach and crawled under the low belly of the machine.

Mustav's booming voice filled the air. "Drop the guns or die!"

Reacting with a speed that spelled long training, two of the enemy seized the pilots and held .45s to their heads. The other two dropped into battle crouches, ready to return enemy fire. The quickness of reaction, the lack of spoken commands—it all added up to mercenary.

Gadgets, still under the belly of the copter, still out of view, pulled the silenced Beretta from its holster. He took a two-handed prone position, lined the sights on a head and waited.

Carl Lyons could now see the barbed wire across the prison camp. Except for those searching the inside of the camp, everyone had departed. He could make out Pol, waiting by the wire, facing out, scanning the horizon. On either side of him stood Zambian athletes, alert, looking for the enemy.

Seconds dragged through Lyons's body like barbed wire dragged over flesh. Time was running out. He looked at a blood-red desert.

"Everyone's left but us." The voice startled him. He turned to see Babette approaching him. "So far none of the athletes have been killed. Some Klansmen, but no athletes."

"Let's keep it that way," Lyons muttered.

Kelly, Babette and Sam Jackson slid under the razor wire while Pol and Lyons covered their escape. Pol was the next to drop to the ground and put himself under the flesh-shredders. Lyons was the last to go. He was up to his chest in the dirt and wire when the area lit up like noon.

16

The pilots were vital, essential if the athletes were to escape death in the desert at the hands of a mercenary extermination force. If the four gunmen managed to extend the hostage situation for three or four minutes, the athletes, the Klansmen and Able Team would be wiped out. Still, Gadgets could do nothing but wait. Wait for the right moment.

From behind him, back near the camp, the Able Team electronics wizard saw a flash that lit up the sky. Gadgets refused to take his eyes off the enemy.

The waiting paid off. One of the killers looked up at the light, another shouted to the athletes and Klansmen at the dunes.

"Throw down your arms or your pilots buy it."

While the goon was shouting, Gadgets sent three bullets in to destroy the head of the other hostage holder. The gunman dropped to his knees, then dropped onto his face, tasting sand only an instant before he tasted death.

Gadgets quickly swung the whispering gun to sight on the second man, whose gun barrel was wavering near the head of the pilot. That killer's speech ended with a 9mm exclamation mark in the temple. He dropped to a sandy death beside his buddy.

Suddenly the dunes were alive with gunfire. The pilots had the good sense to hit the turf. One of the remaining mercenaries stood his ground and fired, dropping a Klansman with a wild shot to the upper leg. The merc was buried in bullets.

The remaining guncock had gone down with the pilots. The two men wrestled with the gunner, forcing his weapon into the sand. Gadgets carefully lined up the shot, taking great pains to save the pilots. He fired. Bull's-eye. Blood marred the man's forehead. The goon's skull was cracked open by a 9mm beanbreaker.

The athletes and the few remaining Klansmen swarmed over the dune. They climbed into the copters. Gadgets went and offered a hand to each of the pilots, helping pull them off the desert floor. They slapped the dust and dirt off their uniforms. They looked shaky. Gadgets gave them a firm hand on the shoulder.

"Need you now, guys. We're counting on you. Get the machines warmed up and off the ground as soon as I say go. The bastards are closing in on us."

The chopper jockeys wasted no time on questions. They kicked up sand as they scrambled for their machines. Gadgets turned back, trying to hurry people onto the choppers.

LYONS WAS UNDER the razor wire when the lights hit him. Pol reacted instantly. He sent a half clip from the Ingram to shatter the floodlights and destroy the television camera under them.

Petra Dix, who had the camera shot out of her hands, screamed.

The men of Able Team could hear voices shouting from close by.

"That way! It came from over there."

Two of the Zambians, who had liberated rifles from dead Klansmen and were waiting to get onto the copter, started to snipe at enemies moving in from the north.

Lyons regained his feet, at the same time instructing.

"Run for it. Run like hell."

Dix was still screaming. As he passed her, Lyons grabbed a handful of hair and lifted her toes clear off the sand. She gasped. Having been shot at, almost killed, and now this...Petra Dix was losing every inch of self-control.

"Bitch," Lyons snapped at her. "Almost got everyone killed."

He let go of her hair and she looked up at him, ready to lodge a raging complaint. Lyons stared her down. She shuddered.

"What are you doing here anyway?" Lyons snarled.

"I was after a story and I seemed to have found one. What's happening?"

Lyons shook his head. There was no way to deflect this woman away from a story. No way.

Two killers in combat fatigues, who had entered the compound minutes earlier, now used Lyons's escape route and crawled under the barbed wire. Rising to their feet over a small dune, they came upon a helpless Petra Dix and a spinning Carl Lyons. Lyons confronted the gunners, snapping off a burst from his combo gun. The weapon did its work, wiping away their faces in a bloody smear. Dix watched the man at work. Her breath grew choppy, her knees began to buckle.

Lyons grabbed her and propelled her toward the disappearing line of retreating allies.

"Catch up and keep low," Lyons ordered.

She tottered after the line.

"Lower. Faster," Lyons prodded, pushing her in the back with the hot gun barrel.

He could hear activity behind him. The paratroopers were taking over the compound, unaware that those once in the compound had left. Lyons knew they would discover the total emptiness of the area within a minute. Then they would be on the warpath to find the athletes, the deserted Klansmen and whoever had killed the KGB moles.

Lyons decided it was time to discourage pursuit. He stopped and turned, plucking three fragmentation grenades from a bandolier. The first one landed over the dune just as two heads appeared over the top of the sand. They collapsed back, screaming, as the grenade blew.

Lyons raised the M-203 and fired the next two grenades farther back. He was rewarded with ear-piercing screams. He turned and took off with a burst of speed.

When Lyons arrived at the helicopters, they were

full. Both were warming up and the pilot of one was waiting to speak to him. Some people were still waiting to board. Lyons looked for his teammates. Pol and Gadgets were holding the area against the most probable directions of attack. Babette, Kelly and Zak Wilson eyed the third quadrant, Mustav and Jackson the fourth.

The pilot reached Lyons at the same time Petra Dix did. Both spoke at once. Lyons slapped in a new clip and then placed a firm hand over Dix's busy mouth.

"Go ahead," he said to the pilot.

The pilot was clearly uncomfortable with his message. "When we turned our radios back on, we were ordered back to base and told to take no further orders from you, sir. Colonel Follet says he's captured a Soviet spy helicopter over American soil."

"I'm real happy for the hero. You intend to dump the passengers?"

"Between you and me—not a chance."

"Copilots seats filled yet?" Lyons asked.

"Saved them for two of you," the man replied.

Lyons turned to Dix. "There's not enough room for everybody on these birds," he said, fanning a hand at the two jam-packed Sikorskys. "Can your chopper take four more?"

She nodded.

A burst of automatic-rifle fire flew high as Gadgets took out a sniper from the top of a dune. Lyons waved Kelly, Mustav and Wilson over. They arrived on the run.

"One of you in each copilot seat. Hold a gun on these jockeys until they unload everyone at UCLA. The extra person—hop on. Now, move."

The trio sprinted for the copter's doors.

"Thanks," the chopper pilot said. "That lets us off the hook." He took off for his machine.

Lyons thrust five grenades into the arms of Petra Dix. "They're getting too damn close for comfort," he snapped. He loaded a sixth into the M-79 and then, as the sandstorm from the chopper blades began to whip around them, he ran back along the way they had come. Dix hesitated for a moment, but when she saw Pol, Gadgets and Babette following, she hastened to catch up to Lyons.

The crest of the dune ahead of them bristled with M-16s. Very few heads showed—the assault rifles were being aimed at the rising helicopters. Lyons's grenade launcher was the first to speak. The other two Able Team members and Babette joined in with their Ingrams, sweeping the crest of the dune, tearing into heads, kicking up sand. Lyons snatched another grenade from Dix's hand. The M-79 boomed again. Two figures straightened up as nerves were blasted by the impact of thousands of wire shards.

Lyons grabbed another grenade.

"Helicopter is over to the right," Dix shouted. But Lyons did not seem interested in the positioning of the copter; his mind and sights were on the enemy. The second chopper lifted like a monster off the desert floor. All Able Team members felt a great sense of relief. The only bodies on the line were those of Babette Pavlovski and Petra Dix—

both volunteers on the war's battlefront—and themselves, professional fighters, a justice-by-fire death squad.

The eastern horizon was bloody with the arrival of the sun. The sky was light. Soon the sun's strength would be unbearable.

Petra Dix watched as Lyons and his cohorts moved straight ahead, into enemy fire. She wondered what the hell she was doing with them. She was covering a story. She did not want to become one.

When Lyons took the last grenade from Dix's carefully kept hands, she turned right and ran. There was a spare camera in the copter. She could take off and use it on remote. She sprinted. Her lungs, unaccustomed to running, heaved madly.

As she scrambled up the side of the dune she remembered that she had the means of transportation for the others. Later, she thought. Later. She topped the dune in a trot and sped down the other side, right into the arms of four men wearing camouflage combat fatigues. Two of the gunners reached out and caught her by the arms.

"Look what dropped in," one said, a sick grin opening up on his sand-swept face.

"Think we've got us a deserter," said another. The pair threw Dix to the ground. She landed with a thud. She realized her time to play reporter was up. This was no longer a game. By leaving Lyons she had left safety. Now she was paying the price.

The four men were not in a good mood. Their asses were on the line. The athletes had escaped. A small team of crack gunners had decimated their ranks. The sun was up and fast becoming blistering. They wanted no more than to kill the enemy that remained and get the hell out of the sandy battlefield.

One of the bastards held a knife to her throat while another searched her for weapons. He grabbed roughly at her crotch, slapped his hands across her breasts. Dix bit her lip trying not to cry. She wanted to scream but the knife at her throat told her not to.

"How many troops over there?" the man with the knife asked.

"Three men and a woman," Dix whispered.

"Bullshit," the other man snarled, slapping her breast with a powerful swat.

"Hon...honest," Dix gasped. "The rest took off in the copters."

One of the men who hadn't spoken yet piped up. "If they've got only four, let's take them and get out of here."

The man with the knife turned Dix onto her stomach. He took the knife and passed it along her spine. She felt nothing more than a light tingle as the knife sliced through her two-hundred-dollar bush jacket and her bra. The goon pulled her jacket and her bra off, leaving her naked from the waist up. "Tie her feet," the man told his companion. "And hands."

The man, grinning a gap-toothed grin, slobbered on the newswoman as he tied her up.

"We'll have some fun when we're through," he drooled.

Dix appealed to the other men. "You can't leave me here. I'll die of exposure."

"Only if a snake don't get you first," one answered.

"I hope you live," another said. "'Cause when we get back we'll make sure you die of something a lot more fun than exposure."

In the rising heat, Petra Dix shivered.

WHEN THE NEWSWOMAN HAD BOLTED away from Able Team, Babette had turned to chase her.

"Don't," Lyons commanded.

Babette returned to her place in their advance on the enemy.

The foursome crested the dune in a line that spread out for twenty feet. Instead of being met by fierce resistance and a storm of bullets, they only encountered three bodies.

Slowly they advanced. One of the men was still alive. He tried playing possum but gave himself away when he twitched as the breeze slapped sand in his face. Pol noticed the movement.

Blancanales stood over the goon. The man had no weapon.

"Which way did they go?"

The man slowly opened one eye, then the other. The supine figure looked up the barrel of Pol's Ingram. He pointed back toward the prison camp. Blood was seeping from various wounds on his body.

"How many?" Pol asked.

The man was silent. Pol brought the conversation back to life with a nudge of his gun.

"Fuck you," the goon screamed, throwing a fist-ful of sand in Pol's face. The Able Team member turned in time to keep the sand out of his eyes. The goon tried to make a run for it. Pol dropped him with three bullets.

Blancanales looked at Lyons and shrugged. "Looks like they're trying to bottle us."

Lyons pointed a course forty-five degrees shy of moving straight back to the camp. "That'll keep us ahead of the cork and move us closer to the dune buggies. That group straight ahead isn't closing in."

"They'll probably try an ambush at the camp," Gadgets said.

The four warriors set off at a stiff jog. At the crest of each dune they threw themselves on their stomachs and crawled over. Each person knew that the sun would soon be rising to deadly heights and that they could not survive long if they allowed themselves to be herded out into the desert.

By the time they peered over the top of the final dune and saw the camp ahead, they were drenched in sweat. They surveyed the scene with slow care, spotting, noting the location of as many of the enemy as they could find. They slid back five feet to whisper, each watching the horizon over the head of the person facing them.

" 'Bout thirty?" Gadgets guessed.

The others nodded in agreement.

"Gotta wonder how many are out there," Pol said. "How many of the bastards are behind us?"

"Only one twin-engine plane," Lyons pointed out.

"No more than thirty behind us," Pol figured.

"Let's take advantage of the fact that the camp was meant to be wiped out," Lyons said. "I'll create a diversion. You three get a couple of buggies out of there."

Lyons started to skirt the camp, looking for the best place to set up a temporary fire base. The other three crawled along a route that would take them as close as possible to the gate of the compound. They finally reached the dune—now slightly flattened by the wind—from which Lyons and Babette had breached the gate the first time they had entered the enemy camp.

"Fence is high," Pol whispered. "Can we all get over?" Babette and Gadgets nodded.

Lyons began his diversion with two HE blasts into the razor wire, about a hundred feet from the gate. The blasts sent sand flying like geysers, leaving a two-foot crawl hole under the sagging accordion wire. The enemy was well trained: while the majority raced to the point under attack, some held the perimeter.

Schwarz and Blancanales, silenced Berettas in hand and Ingrams in tow, fired from the ridge of the dune. They waited until Lyons showed himself and began blasting with the M-16 portion of the over/under gun. The noise made by Lyons covered the faint, deadly coughs of the Berettas.

While the majority of gunners focused their wrath on Lyons, and while the remainder were intent on covering their own fire sectors, Pol and Gadgets quietly opened a small area.

Gadgets took Babette's Ingram and bandolier. The threesome charged down the dune to the gate. Lyons had popped down for the two seconds it took him to change clips. Now he was up again, twenty feet from where he had first revealed himself to the enemy. His second clip cut down anyone careless enough to get away from cover.

Two of the hardmen had the sense to check their flank. Gadgets made them wish they hadn't. He put a burst in each.

Babette rolled over the fence, bounced to her feet, and caught both Ingrams. She shouldered one and spun to cover Gadgets and Pol with the other.

The Able Team members took the fence. They had penetrated enemy ground. They had been spotted.

Gadgets grabbed his Ingram from Babette and greased the closest goon. Blancanales and the gymnastics coach scattered to the area housing the dune buggies. Babette sent out a stream of fire. Blancanales started two buggies.

Opening the gate, Gadgets felt the slight impact of a bullet grazing his flak jacket. Covering fire, now coming from two directions, kept the enemy down and Schwarz alive.

When the two buggies began to move, Gadgets emptied his Ingram at the enemy. There were no easy targets. The gunners were kissing the sand. The clip emptied just as Babette came charging by in a buggy. The Able Team member grabbed the edge of the windshield, kicking his legs up, letting the momentum of the vehicle swing him over the low door and into the passenger seat.

Gadgets barely had his legs tucked in when a blast rocked the compound, almost lifted the buggy from the ground. Two more shock waves rocked them as they sped away under a hail of bullets. Lyons had barely given them time to make a safe sortie before shooting three HEs into the other buggies. The force of the blast and the flying debris did nothing for the aim of the paratroopers left in the compound.

The two roaring buggies, Blancanales playing catch up to Babette's lead, swept around the first dune out of the fire zone. They circled toward Lyons's position. Phase one of the battle plan complete.

The blitz to liberate the two buggies and destroy the rest had taken only two minutes. By the time the two buggies had roared through the open gate, the surly Captain Young had his paratroopers, and the situation, under control.

"There's only one man up there, you pussies. Take him before the buggies reach him."

Two men tore up a small tent and threw it over the wire. Ten men charged over.

Young unhitched a communicator from his belt.

"Curly. You there?"

"Yeah, Cap."

"How far are you from sector eight?"

"In seven. Almost on top of it."

"A lone gunner. Take him out, now!"

"Got it. Out."

Young stopped five more men who were about to charge out over the tent.

"Rescue as many vehicles as you can. They're our only way out."

The men turned and ran toward the blazing buggies. Several had been protected from direct fire by the wreckage of the others. Lyons had laid the grenades along the edge of the closely packed vehicles. Young's men, prepared to annihilate the camp, had wire cutters. They soon had some fence opened up. They worked feverishly to get a few buggies clear before more gas tanks blew.

Young watched his men work. Not bad for Americans, he thought. But they had botched the ultimate plan—to wipe out the Zambian athletes. Young believed six of his KGB training instructors could have done the job right. He tuned in his small transistor and continued to coordinate his force. He shook his head. They had all made the night jump safely—all sixty-two. Now, his best estimate left thirty alive. As far as he could tell, there were only five or six of the enemy left behind when the copters took off. How in hell did they do so much damage, so much killing?

But things would change, Young thought. Things would change.

Young's men were trained American veterans with no place to use their deadly skills. After Nam they could not adjust to the tedium of civilian living. It had taken Young five years and three million of the Kremlin's precious American dollars, but he had managed to recruit and train these social misfits. The idea had been to have both the blacks and the Klansmen found dead, killed by American guns. It would have been a beautiful black mark against America. It would have been a great propaganda coup, especially since, coinciding with the barbaric murder, many black American athletes would be turning their backs on their homeland, moving to Communist countries.

Now this. Now all of this, because of some crack tactical squad. The bastards will pay, Young thought. They'll pay.

Captain Young rounded up nine troopers. The ten men loaded themselves into the five surviving, slightly damaged, buggies and started along the tracks left by the escaping vehicles. The five vehicles spread out in a V-formation, giving them a wide scan and enabling them to proceed at a high speed without throwing sand on each other.

Young was banking on the fact that even if the two enemy buggies managed to break the circle and pick up their friend, they would not be able to break back out in a hurry. Before they could fight their way out, his men would have them. And if they didn't get them, the sun would. The desert was firing up like the blast furnaces of hell. In the heat, the smaller force would expend its energy sooner.

As HE RETREATED from his firing spot near camp, Lyons searched the bandolier. He took out the one remaining grenade, then threw the bandolier away. From here on in he'd put his life on the 5.56-caliber bullets from the M-16 portion of his gun.

Lyons knew his teammates had sprung two buggies.

Lyons knew he had scant seconds before the enemy trying to box him in would meet the troops that had charged out of the camp.

Lyons knew when that happened he'd be caught. Dead in the middle.

Carl Lyons had tried his best to tone down his self-professed craziness; but he had not lost it.

With a grin on his face he turned and ran straight up the dune—back toward the compound.

17

Lyons's boots churned up sand as he sprinted up the side of a dune. He heard the heated grunts and panting of troops running up the other side toward him. Not breaking pace, not even bothering to pull the pin from the grenade in his hand, he threw it over the crest of the dune.

"Grenade," he shouted as he reached the crest.

"Grenade," an enemy echoed from the other side.

Lyons topped the crest as camouflaged bodies dived in all directions to escape the lethal shrapnel they believed was on the way. A good soldier knows that survival depends on instant reflexes. No one noticed the pin was still in the grenade.

Lyons did not slow his pace. His lungs burned in the arid battleground. He let the downhill side of the dune propel his feet. As he ran he emptied the M-79's clip into the fallen troops. They were sitting ducks. Five dead sitting ducks.

At the bottom of the slope he grabbed the grenade and continued up the next slope, a smaller dune. He was almost to the top before six more men, coming in from the far left, got the big blonde in their sights. He heard a bolt click. He dived over the top of the dune, tucking, rolling, halfway to the bottom. As soon as he could gather his feet under him, he pulled the grenade's pin and let the killer fly.

Six men ate sand and shrapnel. Six men died.

Again Lyons, having snatched a fresh clip from his remaining bandolier and slammed it home, took off toward the camp. Lyons had one more cooling pack in his jacket. He was seeping water but had no time to stop. Even in their flak jackets, the men of Able Team were finding the hellish heat hard to combat.

Blancanales heard the shooting above the roar of his machine. He veered toward the sound. The blast made by the grenade helped him to home in on the spot. It was difficult to judge distance by sound in the rolling dunes.

Gadgets saw that Pol's vehicle was changing course, moving toward the camp. Suicide, he thought. But he shouted to Babette, "Swing wider."

The gutsy woman nodded, acted, swinging wider. Gadgets, full of admiration for her driving skills, held on for his life. He knew that in any war the chance of meeting death was high—but he didn't want to meet death as a passenger in a dune buggy.

Politician swept over another dune and surprise-attacked two goons with his vehicle. As they swung to face him, he bounced them off the fender. He continued tightening his spiral until he was headed directly for the camp.

Babette was doing her best navigating in the sandstorm Pol was leaving behind. As they crested another ridge, to the left they spotted the crew that had been trying to box Lyons in. Gadgets turned and managed to empty half a clip at them before they were lost in a cloud of sand behind the buggy. Babette dropped the buggy into the next trough. Schwarz struggled to keep his stomach out of his mouth.

Lyons paused for a second, gasping deep, dry breaths of air. Ahead of him was the prison camp, easily entered now with the tent thrown over the wire. Behind him was the roar of the buggies and the stutter of an Ingram. To his left and closing in fast was another set of buggies. Lyons was pissed. He thought he had shelled the machines into another world. Obviously not.

With a quick glance he could see that his Able Team partners had swung wide into the desert while the enemy had followed the perimeter of the camp. His teammates would not reach him in time to slow down and pick him up. Lyons started running for all he was worth, racing for the tent draped over the razor wire.

Pol swore when he saw what a close race they were running. He swung his Ingram on the sling until it rested across his left forearm. He steered the buggy with his left forearm, keeping the right arm wrapped around the machine pistol. Spotting Lyons, he veered so that his buggy would arc between his buddy and the approaching force.

At the top of the next rise, both Babette and Gadgets got an eyeful of what was happening. Like a seasoned pro Babette swerved harder left to bring the approaching vehicles between themselves and the camp.

Politician spewed sand between Lyons and the enemy. He was having a hard time controlling the speeding machine. He swung the wheel farther left until he was rushing to meet the enemy, aiming to pass between the goons and the camp's razor wire. As he sped past, he fired bursts until the clip was empty. As he passed them, he was ducking low.

Blancanales's shots, in spite of the jouncing, pegged one driver who lost control. The driver, clutching a torn chest, got his passenger hung up in the razor wire. The buggy came to rest in the compound, its engine stalled, its driver dead.

The return shots fired at Pol's speeding form zipped wide and high.

As the enemy battled the sandstorm, and Pol's firestorm, Babette and Gadgets swooped in from the other side. It was a quick sweep—the pair keeping as low as possible, Gadgets remaining in a firing position throughout the pass. Gadgets's Ingram leveled two gunners and spilled the blood of another driver.

By the time the three remaining vehicles—five remaining enemies—recovered from Able Team's one-two punch, they had passed Lyons. The big blond gunner had hit the sand. When the goons passed, he was kneeling, spraying shots as another clip expired.

Lyons didn't wait to see the results. He got back on his feet and took off again, changing clips on the run.

When Pol passed the enemy vehicles, he took his foot off the gas and jammed his thigh against the steering wheel. His other foot disengaged the clutch. The dune buggy quickly lost speed in the sand. By the time it could come to a complete stop, he had changed clips and was resting the Ingram on his lap. He grabbed the wheel in one hand and the shift lever in the other and used the slow speed to make a tight curve. In a quick maneuver, he was speeding after the remaining mobile enemies.

Babette put the machine she was driving into a tight turn that threatened to dump Gadgets onto the sand. He hung on and changed clips only after the course was straightened out. When the gun was ready, he pulled a grenade from his jacket.

"Back to the group on foot," he hollered to Babette.

She corrected their course. Gadgets pulled the pin from the grenade, but did not release the spoon.

The enemy had turned and were now closing in on Lyons from two sides. A single vehicle was closing on his left, two on his right. The tent over the wire was only five feet in front of him. He dived under the nearest part of the tent and brought the M-203 up to face the enemy.

From his low, almost totally hidden position, Lyons could see little of the enemy. But he wasn't shooting for flesh, he was aiming at tires. He sent a careful burst of 5.56mm wreckers through a tire on each of the three buggies.

Pol, who had turned to attack as Lyons hit the turf, could see no sign of Lyons. He headed for the middle vehicle, prepared to battle in a high-speed game of desert chicken.

Suddenly the three vehicles swerved crazily as drivers fought to prevent the buggies from rolling. Blancanales slipped through the ranks without being shot at. The enemy were limping toward the desert, each vehicle minus a tire.

Lyons scrambled out from his hiding place, changing clips on the run. He had only two clips left. They would have to do.

The three enemy vehicles were out of sight. Pol's machine could be spotted in the distance as the Able Team member stood on the brake. The wheels locked and dug into loose sand. Blancanales slammed the shift lever into reverse and started churning back the way he had come. The wheels clutched sand, shot sand, spun free. The engine whined its complaints as Pol kept the pedal to the floorboard. The little bomb shot back over the dune in reverse.

Pol skidded to a dramatic halt in front of Lyons.

"Well, if it ain't the cavalry," Lyons said with a laugh. He vaulted into the passenger's seat.

The sound of a grenade exploding came from the desert.

Pol took off toward the sound.

When the dune buggy driven by Babette crested a dune and swooped down on the remaining foot soldiers, each side was braced for battle. Babette and Gadgets sank low in their seats as the gymnastics coach aimed the machine straight at the seven survivors. Bullets disintegrated the windshield. Others thudded into body metal. One tire blew and Babette had to fight to keep the buggy from rolling on them. The gunfire quickly thinned out as gunners scrambled out of the path of the racing machine.

When they had just passed the line of thugs, Gadgets dropped the grenade. As the enemy turned to lay fire at the retreating pair, the blast tore two of the gunners to bloody pieces and scattered the others.

Babette fought the buggy to a stop just over the crest of a dune. She and Gadgets jumped out and ran back up to the crest. They split, topping the crest about fifteen feet apart. Quickly they laid deadly fire onto the disorganized enemy. Quickly they killed the five remaining guncocks. The bastards had nowhere to hide. They fell under a hail of bullets.

Gadgets sank back into the sand, exhaustion having wrenched nearly every ounce of strength from his body. Babette, looking tired, haggard, flopped down beside him.

After a second of silence, Gadgets swore.

"I was hoping to get one of the goons alive. Wanted to find out what the hell they did with Dix."

"We'll find her," Babette said with a sigh.

"We'd better. She's our ride."

The sudden sound of an approaching buggy brought both of them back on alert. They crept up to peek over the dune. It was Politician and Lyons, scouring the endless dryness for scum.

The duo stopped the buggy.

For a moment no one spoke. Each person was looking at the face of another warrior. They saw the scars of battle, topped with a fine layer of sand. And they saw the worn look of war. None of them liked what they saw. All were grateful they could not see themselves.

Blancanales spoke up.

"Couple carloads with flat tires around here somewhere waiting for the Motor League. Got to find them."

"Anybody seen Dix?" Lyons asked.

No one had.

"Guess we've got some hunting to do," Lyons said.

It didn't take long to find the place where Dix had separated from the party. They proceeded cautiously, Gadgets and Babette on foot, the dune buggy creeping behind them. Lyons stood precariously behind the passenger seat, holding on to the roll bar. All four scanned the dune line for signs of the enemy.

They found Petra Dix and the four remaining paratroopers at the same time, at the same place.

The paratroopers were expecting them.

Captain Young held a Makarov to Dix's head.

"Looking for her?" he spat.

Dix stood beside the man, her exposed upper body raw from its time in the sun and from being forced to lie on the hot desert sand.

The other paratroopers held guns, but no one made a move to shoot. They had seen what Able Team, plus its female gunner, could do. In Dix they had superb bargaining power. They would take the easy way out, with a gun at Dix's head.

"I want one thing," Young said, contempt for the American sharpshooters rich in his voice. "Just give us the buggy."

"What if we don't," Lyons snapped. "What if we take our chances on a shoot-out—a shoot-out we know we'd win."

"Then you'd lose the bitch," Young snarled. And as the word bitch fired from his mouth, he made his fatal mistake. For emphasis, he took the Makarov away from Dix's head—just long enough to snap the muzzle into her breast. And when he was returning the muzzle to her head....

Dix grabbed the goon's arm and with all her strength she pushed the gun away from herself. Turning, she gave the man a solid shot to the testicles, a shot that swiped the air from his lungs, folded him up.

Lyons's lightning-quick reflexes took over. He squeezed the trigger, putting a burst through the skull of the bent-over KGB killer.

Babette, Gadgets and Pol took care of the other three gunners before the bastards could get off a single shot. The four gunmen lay dead on the sand, their bodies now food for the baking sun. Soon they would become bloated, blistered. Perhaps the only fitting end for the puppets of scum.

Able Team, flanked by a gutsy woman who cared and a nervy reporter who had learned more about life in the past hour of living than she had in the past thirty-two years, headed out of the baking hell.

Their job was done.

Complete.

And done in the only way Able Team knew how—*right*.

**Here are some memorable moments from
Able Team #12: *Deathbites:***

The three Able warriors rushed the front door into the reception area. One look at the minced body of a woman told them they were already late.

They ran through the reception area without slowing, turning left to find themselves in a large, open office. Four men and a woman in one-piece coveralls were holding eleven workers captive. Lyons broke to the right, seeking an angle of fire that didn't include noncombatants in the background.

Pol and Gadgets dropped flat in the doorway. Gadgets's Uzi spoke first, a 3-round burst that took the legs out from under the terrorist closest to the hostages.

Blancanales's M-203 spoke next. A single, carefully aimed shot entered a terrorist's left eye and blossomed in a small fountain of gore at the back of the head.

Terrorist bullets, fired in panic, began chopping up the doorway above the Able fighters' heads. That won Lyons time to flank the gunners. He stood where they formed a row of targets, with the captives on one side and the doorway holding Blancanales and Gadgets on the other. The Atchisson Assault 12 shotgun spoke twice with booming authority.

The two goons closest to Lyons disintegrated from the waist up in a barrage of small, red debris.

"Dr. Lao, where do I find her?" Lyons barked at the terrified staff.

His sharp inquiry rallied several workers from their state of shock and bewilderment. Three hands pointed past the reception area. "She's in the end office, third hallway," someone croaked.

"Okay. Now, get out of here," Lyons commanded. He pointed to an emergency fire exit at the end of the room. People began to mill around in confusion instead of clearing the building.

Lyons gave one of the male office workers a hard nudge with the barrel of the Atchisson. Soon the eleven workers were moving quickly toward the nearest exit. Able Team turned and broke for the other side of the building.

The first corridor they encountered had a single guard at one end. She was lounging against the wall at the mouth of the hall, her 16-gauge shotgun pointing down the passageway, keeping victims confined to their offices until they could be questioned. The shotgun was pointing the wrong way.

Gadgets's uzi sent three corrective messages to the terrorist's brain. She died on her feet.

A half-gagged shout of pain came from the next hallway. Able Team rounded the corner on the run. Three terrorists were questioning a prisoner. Two had M-16s slung over their shoulders and were holding the arms of a man in a white coat. A third had the tip of a pump action 12-gauge Marlin Glenfield shoved into the man's mouth. A trickle of blood ran down the victim's chin from where the muzzle had knocked out a tooth.

The three goons were so preoccupied, they never saw the other armed force until Able Team was among them. Lyons thrust the warm barrel of the Atchisson under the questioner's chin.

"Seeing we're playing twenty questions, perhaps you can tell me what this is?" Lyons asked.

The two men who were holding the victim let go and tried to swing the M-16s from their shoulders. Bad move. Blancanales smashed his M-203 into the first one's temple, killing him instantly as fragments of skull lacerated animal brain. Gadgets crushed the other man's windpipe with his fist, leaving the dispenser of terror to roll on the floor, choking on his own tissue and blood.

"How many of you in this building?" Lyons demanded.

His shotgun was thrust under the chin so hard that the man was stretched to the tips of his toes. He tried bringing his shotgun around to bear on Lyons.

"Don't lose your head," Lyons told him.

The shotgun continued to swing. Lyons's finger tightened on the trigger and decorated half the corridor with atomized head.

A cluster of whizzers sent Able Team diving for cover inside one of the offices.

"Reinforcements," Lyons guessed. "You two find Lao. I'll keep the lice off your asses."

"Then cover me," Gadgets told him.

Lyons threw himself on his stomach and squirmed out the door. Before the hail of lead could drop to his level, he sent two blasts from the Atchisson back up the hall. He was rewarded with a chorus of screams from dying, tenderized terrorists.

Blancanales had already comprehended the plan and had an HE grenade with an impact detonator loaded into the launcher. As soon as Gadgets was out of the line of fire, the Able leader fired the grenade into the far wall.

Lyons sent two more discouraging messages up the hallway while both Gadgets and Blancanales crossed the corridor.

Two quick kicks enlarged the hole in the opposite wall, making it easy to climb through. Blancanales and Gadgets found themselves in a lab on the third corridor.

Gadgets tossed a fragmentation grenade up the hallway, to discourage two terrorists who were near the junction with the cross-hallway. As soon as the blast came, he and his companion raced the other way to the last doorway in the hall. There was no door left to worry about. Pol burst into the room, crouched, ready for action.

More...

Babette walked over to the windows and opened them. Her slow controlled walk already had the men excited. Hers was the perfectly conditioned, balanced body of the highly trained athlete.

Babette locked eyes with one of the men as she played with the buttons on her shirt. They came undone with agonizing slowness. Her victim's eyes were riveted on the shirtfront. He was scarcely breathing.

One of the corpses' heels hit the floor with a slight thump, barely audible above the sound of the stereo. Gadgets looked around quickly, but neither man had noticed.

Babette's shirt slipped from her shoulders as slowly as a snake leaving a sunlit rock. Every move was slow, sensuous. Both men were leaning forward.

Gadgets looked around and spotted an office he could reach without coming into the audience's peripheral vision. He yanked the rope off the arms and hoisted the body to his shoulders.

The music floated up to him as he made his way back. Gadgets found it almost impossible not to stop and stare. Babette was fondling herself in time to the music. The muscles on the men's necks were knotted from their excitement.

Gadgets forced himself to turn his back and lean out the window. He took a deep breath of air before signaling Blancanales to slide the next body down the rope.

The body plummeted two stories. Gadgets braced himself and managed to wrap one arm around it as it almost slipped past. The force tore his grip loose from the window ledge, but he managed to stop the body by catching his feet on the window ledge.

Gadgets glanced over his shoulder. The men were about to fall out of their chairs as Babette slowly and sensuously slipped out of her slacks. The last chorus was playing as the two members of Able Team crept back to the window. Babette was gyrating back and forth in time to the music, clad only in a pair of bikini briefs. Her fingers were on her chest, massaging the flesh in time to the music, causing her breasts to move in a sensuous circular motion. Her tongue snaked out wickedly, sliding across her lips.

The music faded and Babette froze in an inviting pose with her arms spread open.

"Terrific," enthused the one who had let her in.

"Ahh, you didn't finish the act," said the other, pointing to the bikini panties she was still wearing.

Babette reached for her shirt, saying, "I went a hell of a lot further than I ever went before. We're supposed to stop at bra and panties."

The tough one stood up for the first time and seized her wrist. He pointed to the sheath, still strapped to her forearm.

"And what the hell is this?" he growled.

Suddenly Babette's voice was no longer friendly. There was steel in it that had not shown before. . . .

Mack Bolan's

ABLE TEAM

by Dick Stivers

Action writhes in the reader's own street as Able Team's Carl "Mr. Ironman" Lyons, Pol Blancanales and Gadgets Schwarz make triple trouble in blazing war. To these superspecialists, justice is as sharp as a knife. Join the guys who began it all—Dick Stivers's Able Team!

"This guy has a fertile mind and a great eye for detail. Dick Stivers is brilliant!"

—*Don Pendleton*

Able Team titles are available wherever paperbacks are sold.

GOLD EAGLE

Mack Bolan's

PHOENIX FORCE

by Gar Wilson

Schooled in guerilla warfare, equipped with all the latest lethal hardware, Phoenix Force battles the powers of darkness in an endless crusade for freedom, justice and the rights of the individual. Follow the adventures of one of the legends of the genre. Phoenix Force is the free world's foreign legion!

"Gar Wilson is excellent! Raw action attacks the reader on every page."

—*Don Pendleton*

GOLD EAGLE

Phoenix Force titles are available
wherever paperbacks are sold.

DON PENDLETON'S EXECUTIONER

MACK BOLAN

Sergeant Mercy in Nam...The Executioner in the Mafia Wars...Colonel John Phoenix in the Terrorist Wars....Now Mack Bolan fights his loneliest war! You've never read writing like this before. Faceless dogsoldiers have killed April Rose. The Executioner's one link with compassion is broken. His path is clear: by fire and maneuver, he will rack up hell in a world shock-tilted by terror. Bolan wages unsanctioned war—everywhere!

GOLD
EAGLE

Available wherever paperbacks are sold.

MACK BOLAN

Terminal Velocity

**The new SuperBolan!
384 pages of electrifying adventure**

Kill Mack Bolan! The KGB's international conspiracy has already infiltrated Stony Man Farm. April Rose, the woman closest to his heart, is dead. His squads of freedom fighters are scattered.

Now Mack Bolan is outlawed. He is framed by the KGB as a political assassin, and the CIA has orders to kill him.

Bolan has precious little time to nurse his grief. He has always known the truth—that the kill-crazy punk in the street and the ice-cold KGB are the same mad dog. The Hydra!

He has no choice but to rise above all sanction and strike at the very heart of the menace.

He must strike at the Kremlin.

This is Bolan's loneliest, deadliest war!

HE'S EXPLOSIVE.
HE'S UNSTOPPABLE.
HE'S MACK BOLAN!

He learned his deadly skills in Vietnam...then put them to good use by destroying the Mafia in a blazing one-man war. Now **Mack Bolan** ventures further into the cold to take on his deadliest challenge yet—the KGB's worldwide terror machine.

Follow the lone warrior on his exciting new missions...and get ready for more nonstop action from his high-powered combat teams: **Able Team**— Bolan's famous Death Squad—battling urban savagery too brutal and volatile for regular law enforcement. And **Phoenix Force**—five extraordinary warriors handpicked by Bolan to fight the dirtiest of antiterrorist wars, blazing into even greater danger.

Fight alongside these three courageous forces for freedom in all-new action-packed novels! Travel to the gloomy depths of the cold Atlantic, the scorching sands of the Sahara, and the desolate Russian plains. You'll feel the pressure and excitement building page after page, with nonstop action that keeps you enthralled until the explosive conclusion!

Now you can have all the new Gold Eagle novels delivered right to your home! ·

You won't want to miss a single one of these exciting new action-adventures. And you don't have to! Just fill out and mail the card at right, and we'll enter your name in the Gold Eagle home subscription plan. You'll then receive four brand-new action-packed books in the Gold Eagle series every other month, delivered right to your home! You'll get two **Mack Bolan** novels, one **Able Team** book and one **Phoenix Force**. No need to worry about sellouts at the bookstore...you'll receive the latest books by mail as soon as they come off the presses. That's four enthralling action novels every other month, featuring all three of the exciting series included in the Gold Eagle library. Mail the card today to start your adventure.

FREE! Mack Bolan bumper sticker.

When we receive your card we'll send your four explosive Gold Eagle novels and, absolutely FREE, a Mack Bolan "Live Large" bumper sticker! This large, colorful bumper sticker will look great on your car, your bulletin board, or anywhere else you want people to know that you like to "live large." And you are under no obligation to buy anything—because your first four books come on a 10-day free trial! If you're not thrilled with these four exciting books, just return them to us and you'll owe nothing. The bumper sticker is yours to keep, FREE!

Don't miss a single one of these thrilling novels...mail the card now, while you're thinking about it. And get the Mack Bolan bumper sticker FREE as our gift!

BOLAN FIGHTS AGAINST ALL ODDS TO DEFEND FREEDOM.

Mail this coupon today!